I0445627

Till Death do us Part

Written by: Lisa S. McKenzie

Copyright © 2011 by Lisa S. McKenzie

All rights reserved. No part of this book may be reproduced, stored, or transmitted by any means—whether auditory, graphic, mechanical, or electronic—without written permission of both publisher and author, except in the case of brief excerpts used in critical articles and reviews. Unauthorized reproduction of any part of this work is illegal and is punishable by law.

This novel is a work of fiction. Any references to historical events; to real people, living or dead; or to real locales are intended only to give the fiction a sense of reality and authenticity. Other names, characters, places, and incidents either are the product of the author's imagination or are used fictitiously, and their resemblance, if any, to real-life counterparts is entirely coincidental.

ISBN: 978-2-011-00013-2

PRODUCTIONS

Contents

Characters

Michael Stevenson- Husband

Kim Stevenson- Wife

Sasha Stevenson- Daughter

Brandon Stevenson- Son

Mr. & Mrs. Thompson

Carrie Tate- Brandon's schoolmate

Stephanie Tucker- Mother

Teddy Tucker- Father

James Tucker

Ms. Teneges- Client

Sheila

Sharon Turner- Girlfriend

Receptionist #1

Karen Tibbs- Girlfriend

Kimmie-Carlotta's Sister

Anthony- Oldest brother

Marcus- Friend

Mark Richardson

Missy

Prosecutor- Kelly Morris

Malik Lebran- Friend

Ron Jackson- Friend

Manager

Cop #1

Police officer Gary

Prosecutor Ms. Morris.

Male caller

Greeter #1

Monisha- Girlfriend

Greeter #2

Wendy- Office Receptionist

Kevin Tucker- Youngest Brother

Charles- Friend

Usher Patty

Pastor James

Judge Williams

Prosecutor Kelley

Defense Attorney Stoker

Detective #1

Detective #2

Officer

Reporter #1

Reporter #2

Nicole

Natasha

Tosha

Customer #1

Customer #2

Customer #3

Security #1

Co-worker #1

Co-Worker #2

Co-worker #3

Stefan

Truck driver

Kelly Tucker- Sister in law

Raymond Jones- Paula's husband

Clerk

Thomas- Colleague

Parent #1

Brian- Colleague

Parent #2

Marsha- Colleague

Parent #3

Michael- Colleague

Valerie - Girlfriend

Billy- Colleague

Vino- Waiter

Miles

Valet #2

Valet #1

Valet #3

Valet #4

School counselor

Keith

Terrell

Tony

Police officer Gary

Security #2

Paula Jones- Nosey neighbor

Dr. Fenham

Dr. Jenkins

Scene 1

Michael and Kim Stevenson live in Santa Barbara, California, in a mansion overlooking a beautiful view. Michael is the owner of a famous law firm named Stevenson & Stevenson LLP. Kim is a stay at home mom, who works part time at her own boutique, named Casual Attire. Kim and Michael have two kids, ten year old Brandon, and seven year old Sasha. Kim and Michael have been married for nine years and are planning on celebrating their ten year anniversary. It's a sunny Sunday morning, the weather outside is roughly 80 degrees; Kim and Michael are lying in bed enjoying each other. Michael rolls over to his wife and kisses her all over her face. He kisses her eyes, nose, cheeks and lips.

Kim- (moans and turns over) Hmm, that is how a woman should be awakened every day.

Michael- (looking at Kim) You know that I love you.

Kim- (smiles) Yes, but I love you more.

> Kim and Michael begin kissing and caressing each other.

Kim- (whispers to Michael in a sexy voice) Make love to me.

> Michael (smiles) he begins to kiss and caress Kim, he undresses Kim and begins kissing her breast.

Kim- (moans) Oh Michael! Oh Michael!

> Before they could do anything else, Sasha, their daughter comes running into their bedroom.

Sasha- (screaming) Mommy! Daddy! She runs in their room and jumps right into bed with them.

Kim- Honey, what is it?

Sasha- I had a really bad dream.

Michael- That's okay Sweetie, we all have bad dreams, it's going to be okay.

Sasha- Ah ah no it's not, I am never going back to sleep again.

Kim- It's okay Sweetie, you are going to be okay.

Sasha- No it's not, I want to sleep in your bed.

Kim- (in a calm voice) Sweetie, you cannot sleep in bed with Mom and Dad.

Sasha- Why not? I am scared.

Kim- What did you dream about?

Sasha- I can't remember, I just know it scared me.

Kim- How old are you?

Sasha- I am seven.

Kim- That's right, you are seven and you are a big girl. You are not going to let a scary dream prevent you from going back into your room.

Sasha- I am scared, Mommy.

Kim- I am going to walk you back to your room, so you can see that there is nothing there.

Sasha- (begins to cry and plead) Mom, please let me sleep with you.

Kim- I can't Sweetie, now you need to be a big girl and go on back to bed. It's 3 o'clock in the morning. Do you want Mommy to walk you back to your room?

Sasha- No! Why won't you let me sleep with you and Daddy?

Kim- (talking softly) Honey, if I let you sleep with us each time you have a bad dream, you will never want to sleep in your room. I want you to enjoy your room and know that even though you had a bad dream, you can still go back to sleep. You have to remember it's only a dream.

Sasha- Do you have bad dreams, Mommy?

Kim- Yes I do sometimes.

Sasha- Do you get scared?

Kim- I do, but I tell myself that it's only a dream and then I feel better. So let me walk you back to your room.

Sasha- Okay.

Kim looks over at Michael and winks.

Kim- Honey, I will be right back.

Michael- (talking to Sasha) You are going to be okay, Sweetie.

Sasha- Thanks, Daddy.

Kim walks Sasha back to her room and tucks her in bed.

Kim- You see, things are going to be just fine, do you want me to keep your night light on?

Sasha- Sure, thanks Mom.

Kim- Oh Sweetie, you are welcome. When you get up I am going to make your favorite breakfast, French toast.

Sasha- (smiles) That will be so cool, Mom.

Kim- I love you.

Sasha- Love you too, Mom.

> Kim walks over to Brandon's room where he is sleeping. Kim smiles as she closes his door. She walks back into her bedroom. As she gets to the door, she begins to do a strip tease for Michael.

Michael- Look at you, you are still sexy after two kids and almost ten years of marriage. So that we do not get interrupted, let's take this to the bathroom.

Kim- Yes that is what I am talking about.

> She rushes to the bathroom. They close the door and begin to make mad, passionate love; Michael is biting Kim's neck, and squeezing her butt.

Kim- (moans) Oh Michael, that is the spot.

> Michael puts Kim on the sink top and begins making love to her.

Kim- (screams out in ecstasy really loud) Oh my God! Oh my God!   Oh Michael!   Oh yes!   Take it!   Take it! Oooooooooooooooo! Aaaaaaaaaaaaaaa! Take all of it Michael!

Michael- Kim you are too vocal, you need to keep it down. The kids are sleeping.

Kim- (out of breath) They can't hear us, they are sleeping. Stop talking and keep on giving it to me.

> Michael continues to make love to Kim and Kim continues to scream at the top of her voice. The kids hear the screams; Sasha gets up and runs over to Brandon's room.

Sasha- (shaking Brandon) Brandon! Brandon! Wake up! Wake up Brandon!

Brandon- I'm not sleeping, what is it Sasha? What do you want?

Sasha- (whispers) Do you hear that noise coming from Mom and Dad's room?

Brandon- I hear something.

Sasha- Listen carefully, do you hear Mom screaming?

Brandon- Yeah I hear loud screaming but I am so tired, I just went back to bed. It's probably nothing. Mom was probably just laughing.

Sasha- That loud Brandon?

Brandon- I don't know. What do you want me to do?

Sasha- We need to go and see if everything is okay.

Brandon- No let's go back to bed. Dad is there, he will take care of it.

Sasha- What if something happened to Dad?

Brandon- Sasha! This is ridiculous, now go back to bed.

Sasha- No Brandon, listen, Mom is still screaming. Something is wrong, let's go and find out.

> The both run to their parent's room, they didn't even knock on the door, they just open it, but there is no one in the bed.

Brandon & Sasha- (nervous) Mom! Dad!

> Brandon looks at the bathroom, he walks over to open the door but the door is locked.

Brandon- (hesitant) Mom! Dad!

> Kim puts her hands over her mouth.

Brandon- Mom, can you hear me? Why is the door locked? What is going on?

Michael- Kids, your mom is fine; everything is fine.

Kim- (out of breath) Everything is fine Honey, go back to your room.

Brandon- We heard screams, are you okay?

Michael- So did we.

Kim- (whispering) Michael! Don't be silly. Honey, your dad is here with me everything is fine.

Sasha- What's going on? Why were you screaming? Why is the door locked?

Kim- (looks at Michael) Say something.

Michael- Your mom fell and I think she hurt her leg. I am trying to see if she broke something.

> Brandon (puzzled) looks at Sasha.

Brandon- But why is the door locked?

Michael- Look, stop asking so many questions. Your mom and I are fine so go on back to bed.

Sasha- No I want Mom.

Kim- Sasha Sweetie, Mommy is fine; Daddy is taking good care of me so go on back to bed, okay?

Sasha- Are you sure?

Kim- Yes Honey, I am positive. Now go on back to your room.

Sasha- (looks at Brandon) I guess we need to go back to our rooms.

Brandon- I guess so, Mom sure is acting weird.

>The kids walk back to their rooms
>Kim and Michael come out of the shower, grab their robes and walk into the bedroom. The phone rings.

Michael- Who the hell is calling us so damn early in the morning?

Kim- I don't know but let me go and get it.

Michael- No, let it go to voice mail.

Kim- No I should get it. It could be an emergency.

Michael- Yeah, it's probably your parents. They always have an emergency.

>Kim rolls her eyes and she puts on her robe. She goes to answer the phone,

Kim- Hello.

Stephanie- How are you, Sweetie?

Kim- (surprised) Mom! Do you know what time it is?

Stephanie- Yes, I am calling aren't I? It's morning time, you and that lazy husband need to get up.

Kim- Mom, it's too early for the attacks. What is going on? Is everything okay with you and Dad?

Stephanie- Yes of course. Your dad and I are going for our daily morning walk; you and that lazy husband should try that sometimes.

Kim- Mother please! I do not have time for this. What do you want?

Stephanie- First of all you need to watch your tone with me okay.

Kim- Mom, I am serious.

Stephanie- I am serious, too. Where are my grandbabies?

Kim- Sleeping Mom, what do you think?

Stephanie- You see? You are raising those kids wrong, if a 65-year-old woman and a 60 year old man can get up at 7 o'clock in the morning on the weekend, so could those kids. You and that no good husband are raising my grandbabies the wrong way.

Kim- I am warning you Mom, one more comment about my husband and I am hanging up.

Stephanie- You won't dare. Look, I know that Sasha's birthday is next week and wanted to find out what were you doing for her.

Kim- I am not sure yet, I am trying to deal with today. I can't be into next week right now.

Stephanie- You know, there is too much negative energy coming through this phone, so I will call back later.

Kim- (annoyed) Yeah do that, Mom.

Stephanie- Make it a great day, Kimber.

> Kim hates when her mom calls her that, it's usually when she is being sarcastic. Kim hangs up the phone with out saying bye. Michael lies in bed shaking his head.

Michael- I knew it, I had a feeling it was your mother.

Kim- She is so ridiculous sometimes.

Michael- What did she want?

Kim- Nothing as usual. I might as well get up and start breakfast.

> Kim walks to the bathroom and brushes her teeth, Michael follows her and does the same.

Kim- Are you going to church with us?

Michael- No, I am going to the gym and then to the office to work on my current case.

Kim- I can't wait for that case to be over.

Michael- Me too.

> They both laugh. She puts on a tee shirt and some shorts. Kim walks to Sasha's room, and Sasha is watching television. Kim walks over and kisses her on the cheek.

Kim- Good morning, Sunshine. How did you sleep?

Sasha- I slept okay, could have been better if I were in your bed.

Kim- Yeah okay, are you ready for breakfast?

Sasha- Yes.

Kim- Good, I will give you a call when it's ready. Don't forget to wash your face and brush your teeth.

Sasha- (looking at her mom's leg) So are you okay?

Kim- Yes, Honey I am fine.

Sasha- How is your leg?

Kim- My leg, what leg? There is nothing wrong with my leg.

Sasha- Remember, you were screaming out really loud and when we came to your bathroom door, Dad said you were screaming because he thought you broke your leg.

Kim- Yes, oh yes. I fell but my leg is fine.

> Kim quickly walks out of Sasha's room and into Brandon's room. Brandon is playing video games.

Kim- Good morning, Handsome.

Brandon- Hi Mom.

> Kim walks over and kisses him on his cheeks.

Kim- How did you sleep?

Brandon- Other than being awakened by loud screams, I guess I slept well.

Kim- (smiles) Okay smarty-pants, you got jokes ha.

Brandon- (smiling) Okay, Mom. So how are you feeling? How is the leg?

Kim- Oh it's a bit sore but I will be fine.

Brandon- How did you fall?

Kim- I was reaching for something.

Brandon- Well good to know you are fine. You seem to be walking fine though.

Kim- What do you want for breakfast?

Brandon- Whatever you fix Mom, I will eat.

Kim- That is what I am talking about, a kid that is not hard to please. I will call you when it's ready.

> Kim gets up from the bed and limps a little as she walks out the door.

Brandon- (looks at her as she walks away and says) Thanks Mom, you are the best mom ever.

Kim- (turns around and smiles) You just made my day, Son.

> Kim heads downstairs to prepare breakfast. Michael walks over to the kids' room as well; he enters Sasha's room first, since it's the closest to their room. He enters the room; Sasha is in her pajamas watching cartoons.

Michael- Hello Sunshine, how are you this morning?

Sasha- Daddy, I am much better now.

Michael- How did you sleep?

Sasha- I slept okay.

Michael- You see, it was not as bad as you thought.

Sasha- Nope.

Michael- Good, I am glad to hear that.

Sasha- Daddy, can I ask you a question?

Michael- Sure anytime, what's up?

Sasha- Is Mommy okay now?

Michael- Yes Honey, why do you ask?

Sasha- Well she was screaming so loud as if she were in pain. So I was just checking.

Michael- (smiles) Oh your mom is okay.

Sasha- Is her leg better?

Michael- Her leg? There is nothing wrong with your mom's leg.

Sasha- You remember Daddy, you said Mom fell, and you were trying to see if she broke her leg.

Michael- Yes, oh yes, no your mom did not break her leg, she just bruised her leg.

Sasha- I am sure you took good care of her right, Daddy?

Michael- (smiles) Yes, Daddy took good care of her. Where is your brother?

Sasha- In his room.

Michael- (kisses her on the cheeks) Okay Sweetie, I will see you downstairs in a few for breakfast.

Sasha- Okay, Daddy.

> Michael walks over to Brandon's room; Brandon is still playing his video game.

Michael- (enters the room, he walks over to Brandon) What game are you playing, Son?

Brandon- Hey Dad, I am just playing my usual Punk'd. So you want to play?

Michael- No, your dad is tired of getting beat by you.

Brandon- Practice makes perfect.

Michael- Okay, let's do it.

> Michael and Brandon begin to play the video game; Kim is downstairs in the kitchen preparing breakfast. Sasha comes running into the kitchen.

Sasha- Mom, do you need help?

Kim- Yes, you can set the table.

Sasha- (excited) I can do that.

Kim- Honey call your brother and Dad; let them know that breakfast is ready.

Sasha- Okay (she runs to the bottom of the stairs and call out to them) Brandon! Dad! Breakfast is ready.

Michael- Thanks Honey, we will be right down.

> Michael is actually getting beat at the game by Brandon.

Michael- Darn I can't believe I did that.

Brandon- (smiling) I can.

Michael- Darn it.

Brandon- Yes I won. I love beating you, Dad.

Michael- I was really close this time. You only beat me by five points. Oh well let's go downstairs and see what your mom has for breakfast.

> Brandon and Michael head downstairs. Sasha is still setting the table. Michael walks over and kisses Kim.

Michael- Something smells good up in here.

Sasha- Yep that is Mom's French toast and pancakes.

Kim- You all sit down.

> Everyone sits down at the table, they hold hands
> and Michael says Grace.

Michael- Thank You Lord, for this special day. Thanks for waking us up this morning, thank You for the lovely breakfast, thank You God, Amen.

> Everyone says Amen.

Kim- (turns to Sasha) What can I get you, Honey?

Sasha- I want two pieces of French toast, and two pancakes.

Kim- What would you like to drink?

Sasha- OJ please.

Kim- Coming right up. What about you Brandon?

Brandon- Two pancakes and two pieces of French toast, and I would love milk please.

Kim- Okay and what about you Michael?

Michael- (looks at Kim up and down in a flirtatious way) I will eat anything you give me, Honey.

Kim- (smiles) Come on you all, let's eat. I have a busy day.

Michael- I am going to have a little bit of each. I have a long day, so I am going to eat real fast and then run.

> Michael walks over and kisses Kim on the lips.

Michael- Have a good day in church. Kids be good to your mom, I love you.

Kim- How long will you be at the gym?

Michael- Probably two hours, if you need me just call me on my cell.

Kim- Okay.

Brandon- Bye Dad.

Michael- See you all later. Have a great service.

Kim- Hurry up guys we have to get ready for church, it's Easter Sunday and you know how crowded it gets.

Brandon- Mom, do we have to go?

Kim- Brandon, what kind of a question is that? Of course you have to go.

Brandon- It just seems that everyone in church is so fake, it's not genuine. I really do not enjoy going.

Kim- Brandon that is not for us to judge. We can't be concerned with others. We just have to make sure we are not fake.

Sasha- Mom, can I wear my pink dress?

Kim- Of course you can. You all need to go upstairs and take a shower.

> The kids head upstairs and Kim puts the dishes in the dishwasher.
> Michael heads out of the door and walks towards his Porche. Their next-door neighbor Paula is doing her usual peeking. Paula is peeping out of her bathroom window. Michael gets into his car; he puts in the Best of Miles Davis; his phone rings.

Michael- Hello.

Malik- Man, where you at? You are late as usual.

Michael- I am en route, I should be there in 10 minutes, how long have you been there?

Malik- I got here half an hour ago.

Michael- Okay, I will see you shortly.

Malik- Peace.

Scene 2

Michael pulls up at Gold's Gym. He passes by the receptionist, Candy.

Candy- (in a flirting voice) Well hello Michael, if it isn't the sexiest man in the gym.

Michael- Hello Candy, how are you?

Candy- I am good now that you are here. (she throws him a towel) Have a good workout Michael; let me know if there is anything, I mean anything, I can do for you.

Michael- Thanks Candy, but I'm good.

> Michael walks past two women who are seriously getting their free weights on. He then passes by folks on the treadmill; he walks into the weight room and he sees Malik. Malik is lying on his back doing his bench presses.

Michael- What's up, Man?

Malik- (gets up and walks over to Michael and gives him a hand shake and a hug) What's up, glad you can make it.

Michael- Yeah Man, yeah.

Malik- How is the family?

Michael- They are great. I am so fortunate to have a woman like Kim and my two kids.

Malik- That's great Man; you have one of the best marriages known to man.

Michael- Thanks Malik. How are you and Karen?

Malik- Don't even ask, Man.

Michael- What? I thought you all were going to counseling.

Malik- We did, but I think she wants out, Man; I think she has fallen out of love with me.

Michael- Come on Man, don't be ridiculous. Karen did not fall out of love.

Malik- Well what do you call it? We have the twin girls and Josh. I tell you it's breaking Josh's heart. The girls are too young to know what is happening, but Josh is ten and he knows what's up.

Michael- Come on now, 12 years of marriage, three beautiful kids, it's worth the fight.

Malik- I totally agree, but it takes two. Karen has given up on us Man, and that shit hurts; it hurts like hell.

Michael- Well what do you think it is? You think she got someone else?

Malik- She says no, but I have a feeling she has someone else. She says I work long hours and I ignore her, and she does not feel she is getting what she needs.

Michael- What?! I can't believe that. You all have three kids, when will she have time to cheat?

Malik- Look I don't know, Man. All I know is that we have not had sex in five months.

Michael- (shocked his voice gets loud) Five months of no sex!

A few people in the gym turn around and look.

Malik- Yeah, tell the entire gym.

Michael- Man, are you serious?

Malik- Yes Man, I am going to burst.

Michael- Sounds like she is the one with the issues Man, she just needs to decide what she wants to do.

Malik- Okay, enough about my problems. Let's get our work out on.

Michael- I'll spot you.

Michael grabs the weights so that Malik can do his bench presses.

Malik- Good, put 50 on each side.

Michael- Are you sure? I know that you are under stress, but let's not kill ourselves here.

Malik- (laughs) Man, just add the weights.

Michael adds the weights and Malik does his reps; he finishes up and them Michael takes his turn. And they rotate. Michael finishes his rep; they both look at their watches.

Malik- Boy, that was some workout.

Michael- Yes, it was.

Malik- I need to get out of here; I have to pick up my kids.

Michael- Same place and time next week?

Malik- You got it.

Both men walk out of the gym.

Candy- How was the workout guys?

Malik- Great!

Candy- You both look great. I guess I will be seeing you all next week.

Michael- I guess.

Candy- Take care guys.

Michael and Malik walk out of the gym talking.

Malik- Man that was a great workout.

Michael- (grabbing his towel) Yes sir it was.

Malik- I have to pick up my kids but I do have 45 minutes to spare, do you want to grab something to eat?

Michael- I would, but I want to surprise Kim. She and the kids are at church and I want to have dinner already prepared for them when they return home.

Malik- Man that is beautiful, I love what you and Kim have.

Michael and Malik hug.

Malik- Man, I am going to catch up with you later.

Michael- Yes do that, maybe you, Karen, Kim and I can have lunch sometime.

Malik- Yeah, maybe.

Michael- Talk to you later.

Malik- Peace.

Scene 3

Kim and the kids leave the house and head off to church.

Sasha- I saw Ms. Paula staring out of her bathroom window when we were leaving.

Kim- You should have waved to her.

Brandon- Mom, she is so creepy. Why does she spy on us all the time?

Kim- I have no idea, she obviously does not have a life.

> They drive to church; there are so many parked cars that the cars are practically piled up upon each other.

Kim- Wow! Church is packed to capacity. Looks like we will have to park farther away from the church.

> Kim and the kids walk towards the church; there are two greeters waiting to greet them in front of the church.

Greeter #1- Here comes Mrs. Stevenson and her kids.

Greeter #2- I wonder what is going on with her and her husband? He has not been accompanying her to church.

Greeter #1- Yes it has been a good month or so since we've seen them together.

Greeter#2- Sounds like there is trouble in the household.

Greeter #1- Aah ha.

Greeter #2- She tries to come up in here all dressed up acting like everything is fine, I know that she is hurting.

Greeter #1- She looks like she has lost some weight; she looks awfully skinny to me.

Greeter #2- Yeah, she does not look so hot.

> Both greeters smile as Kim and the kids get closer up the stairs. Kim and the kids reach the top of the stairs.

Greeter #1- (with a big smile on her face) Good morning Mrs. Stevenson, don't you look lovely today.

Kim- Thank you.

Greeter #2- Where is that husband of yours? Working as usual?

Kim- As a matter of fact, he is.

Greeter #2- (turns to the kids) Look at you two, you all look so lovely, and are growing so lovely.

Sasha- Thanks.

Greeter #1- Enjoy the service.

> Kim and the kids walk into the church; another usher comes over and hugs Kim.

Usher Patty- Good morning Kim, how are you this morning?

Kim- I am doing great, thanks for asking.

> Usher Patty, ushers Kim and the kids to their seat. The choir is singing, *God Is Going To Work It Out*, folks are clapping and dancing, some are waving their hands in the air and some are dancing in the aisle. Kim and the kids join in with everyone singing and clapping. The song is over and the pastor gestures everyone to take his or her seat.

Pastor James- He is a good God you know. If you know that He is a good God stand up on your feet and give Him some praise.

> The entire congregation gets up on their feet and begins to clap.

Pastor James- Yes, He is a good God and an on time God. Thank Him right now for all that He has done for you, thank Him for waking you up this morning, and thank Him for clothing and feeding you. Thank Him.

> The entire congregation gets up and are clapping their hands, some are saying thank You Jesus, and some have their hands in the air waving a sign of thanks to God.

Pastor James- Please be seated. Good morning Church.

Congregation- Good morning.

Pastor James- I don't know about you but I am happy this morning, I am happy that the Lord saw fit to wake me up.

The congregation clap their hands.

Pastor James- I am happy that He is a forgiving God. I am happy today that He is an awesome God, He is more than enough.

> The choir begins singing the song, *More Than Enough*, He's more than enough more than enough for me.

Pastor James- Does anyone here today want to testify of how God has been more than enough for you? I know that He has been more than enough for me. Yes He has.

> Ten folks raised their hands; an older woman comes to the front to testify.

Older Woman- Good Morning, Church.

Congregation- Good Morning.

Older Woman- It's good to be in the house of the Lord today. I want to testify two years ago today, I was laid off from my job of 40 years. After I got laid off I got sick and I had to deplete all of my savings. Can someone say deplete?

Congregation- (says) Deplete.

Older Woman- My complete savings were gone. I lost my house, my car, and myself. My friends and family turned their backs on me, literally. So I had to turn to the streets. I lived on the streets for two years. I thought I was dead; I felt dead. I never stopped praying, even on the streets I kept on praying and thanking God for keeping me alive. I felt He was keeping me alive for a reason.

Congregation- (some in congregation are saying Amen some saying thank You Jesus, Hallelujah)

Older Woman- Then one day there was the annual walk for the homeless and someone in the shelter asked me if I would be interested in participating. I said absolutely. At that walk I met a reporter who asked me how I became homeless; he asked me what I was doing before. I told him I used to be a Vice President of Human Resources and was laid off, took ill and lost everything. He could not believe it. He said let me help you. I thought he was going to give me a few dollars, but instead he helped me find a job and a place to live. I just want to testify today that whatever you are going through, remember there is a God up above looking down, and He will never forsake you, just believe in Him and He will see you through it, it does not matter if it takes one month or one year, just keep the faith and never stop praying.

> The congregation stands up and begins to clap, some are saying yes Lord, some are saying thank You Jesus. The older woman starts getting the Holy Ghost and talking in tongues and jumping up and down, the congregation continues to clap.

Pastor James- He is a good God you know; if you know that He is a good God stand to your feet and give God the praise.

> Everyone in the church stands up and is clapping, some people are crying, some are catching the Holy Ghost.
> The choir begins to sing He has set me free, He has set me free, I will rejoice that He has set me free.

Scene 4

Kim and the kids leave church and are on their way home. Kim stops briefly at her parent's house since it's on the way.

Kim- (talking to the kids) Hey kids, we are going to stop by your grandparent's for a quick minute to say hello, okay?

Sasha- Cool.

Brandon- Not a problem.

> Kim pulls up in the driveway of a beautiful five bedroom colonial style brick home, with its three car garage and so much land that you can build two other homes, one in the back and one in front. Kim rings the doorbell. Teddy Tucker is sitting in the living room watching a football game, his wife Stephanie is in the kitchen chatting with their younger son Kevin. Kim rings the bell a second time.

Teddy- Who the hell is it? It's Sunday afternoon for crying out loud and we are not expecting any company.

The doorbell rings a third time.

Brandon- Mom, maybe Grandma and Grandpa are not home.

Kim- (annoyed) They are home, they are just being lazy.

Teddy- (yells out to his wife) Honey, can you get the door please? I am watching a game.

Stephanie- (looks at Teddy and shakes her head) Sure, I will get it since you are so busy.

> Kevin, Kim's brother is visiting. His cell phone rings and he goes out to the backyard to answer it.

Teddy- It's probably those Jehovah witnesses, I am getting so tired of them.

> Stephanie walks to the door and looks out of the peephole.

Stephanie- (excited) Ooooh, it's my grandbabies.

> Stephanie opens the door.

Kim- Hi Mom.

Stephanie- Look at my precious grandbabies, come here and give Grandma a hug.

> Both Sasha and Brandon go over and give their grandma a hug.

Stephanie- How are you all doing? Your granddaddy and I miss you all, you know we do not see you all that much.

Kim- Ma, stop it.

Stephanie- Stop what? I am just keeping it real; we don't see our grandbabies often.

Kim- See, this is the reason I don't stop by sometimes.

Teddy- (yelling from the living room) Stef, who is it?

Stephanie- It's your grandbabies and Kim.

> Teddy gets up from off the couch and practically runs to greet the kids.

Sasha- Grandpa! (as she jumps into his arms)

Teddy- How are you sweetie?

Sasha- I am great.

Teddy- Grandpa has something for you.

Kim- Dad, please stop with the gifts, it's not necessary.

Teddy- (looks at Stephanie) Who does she think she is talking to?

Stephanie- Can't be you, she knows better.

> Teddy reaches in his pocket and pulls out a $100 bill and gives it to Sasha.

Sasha- (excited) Oh Grandpa thank you, I am going to put this in my savings account.

Teddy- Good. (he looks at Brandon) Come on over here, Handsome.

Brandon- (goes over and hugs Teddy) How are you, Grandpa?

Teddy- I am great now that you are here, now I have a little something for you as well.

Brandon- Grandpa, you don't have to.

Stephanie- Did your father tell you not to take money from us, Brandon?

Brandon- No.

Stephanie- Yes he did, I tell you he is trying to turn our grand-babies against us.

Kim- Mom! You stop it right now.

Stephanie- Stop what? I am just telling the truth.

Teddy- Boy you are my only grandson, and I like giving you and your sister presents. You hurt Grandpa's feelings when you say no.

Brandon- I'm sorry Grandpa, I did not mean to hurt you.

Teddy- That's okay now take this. (he gives Brandon $100 bill)

Brandon- Wow! Thanks, Grandpa.

Kim- Dad, that is really not necessary.

Teddy- Girl, who are you talking to? Those are my grandbabies that I rarely see, so if I want to give them money I will.

Brandon- Oh Grandpa, that is awesome, thanks.

Stephanie- Kids, are you hungry?

Kim- Mom, you know that I cook every Sunday, we just came by to say hello.

Stephanie- That has nothing to do with me asking if the kids are hungry.

Kim- They are not, plus we are going home to have our usual Sunday dinner.

Teddy- You know Kim, I do not like the way you speak to me, and so you had better watch your tone, Girl.

Kim- No disrespect Dad, but I am sick and tired of you and Mom talking bad about Michael, especially in front of my kids.

Teddy- Michael! Who is Michael? Who said anything about Michael?

Stephanie- Oh your husband Michael, see Honey, the truth hurts, and you just do not like hearing the truth about that no good husband of yours.

Kim- That is it, I am out of here. I will not let you disrespect my husband and my kids' father in front of me nor them. It's ridiculous! That is the exact reason we do not come by often.

Stephanie- (looks at Teddy) Who is she talking to like that? I know she is not trying to get loud with me in my house.

Kim- (upset) Where are the kids? We are so out of here.

Stephanie- They are out back with their uncle Kevin.

Kim- Kevin is here? Why didn't you all tell me Kevin was here? When did he get here?

Teddy- If you had shut your mouth and stopped talking back to us we would have told you your brother is here.

Stephanie- He is just passing through; his band will be performing at Fox nightclub this weekend, so he is here.

Kim- Where is he now?

Stephanie- He is in the backyard.

> Kim is so excited she runs out back to say hello
> to Kevin. As she walks to the back Kevin is
> hugging and playing with Sasha and Brandon.

Kevin- You all have gotten so big. What are you all up to?

Brandon- Well I am playing soccer now, and I run track.

Kevin- That is great! Quite the athlete.

Brandon- (blushing) Well I try.

Kevin- What about you, Sasha?

Sasha- I am taking ballet classes and I also take piano lessons.

Kevin- That is so good, I am very proud of you both.

> Kim comes running in the back, she is screaming
> out. The kids go back in the house.

Kim- Kevin! Kevin! (She runs to hug him) Kevin it's so good to see you.

Kevin- You too, Little Sis.

> They hug for a good two minutes.

Kim- You don't even call me like you used to.

> They are still hugging each other.

Kevin- Well being on the road it's hard sometimes.

> They both sit down on the bench out back.

Kim- So fill me in, what has been going on with you?

Kevin- Nothing much.

Kim- Oh don't give me that, the last time I saw you, you and your girlfriend Melissa were engaged. So give me the details.

Kevin- There are no details to tell.

Kim- Oh come on Kevin, stop holding out. I want details. Have you all set a date? Eloped? What?

Kevin- (sighs) No Kim, nothing like that happened.

Kim- So tell me, what's up?

Kevin- Melissa and I broke up.

Kim- (surprised) Oh no Kevin, I am so sorry to hear, what happened?

Kevin- It was just not working out.

Kim- You all have been together for four years and you all were engaged, so what really happened?

Kevin- Like I said it was just not working out.

Kim- Did she cheat on you? Ooh if she cheated I would (before Kim could finish Kevin interrupts her)

Kevin- Look, I do not want to talk about it.

Kim- What is the matter with you? This is your Little Sis here, we have shared so much in the past, so don't hold out now. Come on give me the details. Who are you dating now? I need a name.

Kevin- You don't quit do you?

Kim- You and I used to be so close. We told each other every-thing. What happened to that? Why can't we talk openly?

Kevin- I just do not want to talk about who I'm dating.

Kim- Okay, but you are dating someone else?

Kevin- (smiles) Yes.

Kim- (excited) Oooh tell me about her? What is her name?

Kevin- You are something else. I guess you did not hear me when I said I did not want to talk about this.

Kim- I have always been your confidant and you know you can tell me anything. Why are you holding back and being secretive? You know all of my secrets so what's up. So come on I need a name.

Kevin- Tracey.

Kim- Hmm Tracey, cute. Okay describe her, is she tall, short, white black come on tell me all about her.

Kevin- (sighs and he gets up from the chair and walks around) Look, I don't want to talk about it.

Kim- Why not? Come on Kev, stop holding out. Tell me about her.

Kevin- (sighs) Kim, please.

Kim- Kevin, come on tell me about her.

Kevin-It's not a her.

Kim- (shocked) What? What did you just say to me?

Kevin- Tracey is not a girl.

Kim- Okay Kevin, funny. Now come on and be serious. Tell me all about Tracey.

Kevin- I'm serious, Tracey is not a girl.

Kim- (looking puzzled and confused) Then what is she?

Kevin- (pauses for awhile) Tracey is a guy.

Kim- (shocked and angry, she gets up from off the bench) A guy? What did you say?

Kevin- I said Tracey is a guy.

Kim- Come on Kevin, stop playing.

Kevin- I'm not playing.

Kim- What the hell are you saying then Kevin?

Kevin- You see? I know I should not have told you.

Kim- Kevin stop playing; Kevin tell me you are playing.

Kevin- (with a serious look on his face) I am not joking. I am in love with a man.

Kim- (begins yelling and screaming) That is ridiculous Kevin! How could you?

>   Stephanie hears the screaming and looks out of the window.

Stephanie- (calls out to Teddy) Teddy! Teddy!

Teddy- Stephanie what the hell is it?

Stephanie- Come here for a second.

Teddy- I am watching a game and do not have time.

Stephanie- (in a stern voice) Teddy, you had better get over here right now.

Teddy- This had better be good.

>   Teddy walks over to where Stephanie is standing in the kitchen.

Teddy- What is it?

Stephanie- Look out the window, what do you think is going on? Looks like they are arguing and Kim is blatantly upset.

Teddy- (looks out the window, Kim is pointing her fingers in Kevin's face, Teddy can hear them yelling) Looks like they are arguing Stephanie, most siblings do that.

Stephanie- No this looks serious; read their body language, something is going on. He is telling her something and she is crying. They are both crying.

Teddy- You need to stop being nosey, they are two siblings disagreeing about something that I do not particularly care to know about.

> Teddy walks back to the living room to watch his game; Stephanie continues to watch Kevin and Kim out back.

Kim- How could you?

Kevin- How could I what?

Kim- How could you do this to your family? Are you crazy? What the hell is wrong with you?

Kevin- Why does something have to be wrong with me Kim? What is so wrong with loving a man?

Kim- (screaming) Everything is wrong with it. It's sick. It's not normal, it's not right.

Kevin- By whose standard, Kim? Society.

Kim- I don't want to talk about it, this is crazy. You need help.

Kevin- (angry) I need help, I need help. You know what I should not have said anything. I knew that Mom and Dad would not understand, but I thought you would.

Kim- (angry) You expect to me understand that you are gay? You are asking for too much. I can't. It is despicable. What happened to all the girls that you brought home? What, they were not good enough?

Kevin- I don't need to explain myself to you.

Kim- Well, you will have to explain it to Mom and Dad.

Kevin- No I do not. I am a grown ass man and I don't need anyone's approval.

Kim- So what are you going to tell them?

Kevin- Nothing, it's none of their business.

Kim- It's none of their business? Kevin you cannot go on lying to them.

Kevin- I am not lying to anyone, but the whole world does not have to know my business. And if you tell them I swear I will never forgive you.

Kim- So what do you want me to do? Lie?

Kevin- I am not asking you to do anything. I shared something with you in confidence and I hope you will respect that. Is that asking too much?

      Kim begins to cry.

Kevin- Great! This is what I need right now.

Kim- (crying) Why, Kevin? Why?

Kevin- I don't have a reason as to why I am attracted to men. I always have been.

Kim- (yelling) No! No! That is a lie that is what you are telling yourself, trying to convince yourself. What about Melissa, Camilla, Sharon and Tiffany? Were they all lies?

Kevin- Yes I used them to camouflage my secret. I tried to fight it. I tried to date women to see if they made me happy but they did not. I don't want to hide anymore; I've hidden it for too long.

Kim- (sobbing) I can't believe what I am hearing, this is not right. Oh my God why? She cries out even louder.

Kevin- (with tears in his eyes) I did not mean to hurt you or anyone. This is who I am and I hope you can accept me for me. I am still Kevin I am still your big brother who loves you very much. Nothing has changed on my end, but I'm afraid what I just shared with you has changed your view of me. (he wipes a tear from his eyes)

Kim- (crying) I will try to understand Kevin, but I can't promise anything. I still love you. I am just confused that's all. It hurts, that's all. Can you understand that?

Kevin- I understand, but I am still Kevin.

Kim- I know.

Kevin- Stop crying. (he reaches out to give her a hug)

> Kim sobs in his hand. Stephanie decides to go out side to find out what is going on.

Stephanie- Okay you two, what is going on out here? Why are you both crying?

> Kim tries to wipe her eyes real fast.

Kevin- Everything is fine Mom, we were just catching up on old times, isn't that correct Kim?

Kim- Yes, that is correct.

Stephanie- Are you all hungry? I can fix you both something.

Kim- No Mom, I have to get going. I need to go home and prepare dinner.

Kevin- I am okay Mom, I need to be leaving soon for rehearsal.

Stephanie- Okay.

> Stephanie goes back inside.

Kim- (hugs Kevin) It was good seeing you.

Kevin- Are you sure about that?

Kim- Yes smart-ass. Even though I am still in shock and a bit angry with you for your choice, I still love you.

Kevin- Love you too. Now promise me Kim you will not say anything to anyone about our conversation.

Kim- I promise.

Kim- I have to get going. Where are you staying?

Kevin- At the Ritz Carlton.

Kim- Okay, call me later.

Kevin- I will.

> They hug each other again.

Kim- I love you.

Kevin- Love you, too.

> They both walk inside the house. Kim walks into the living room where Teddy and the kids are sitting watching the game.

Kim- Come on kids, it's time to go.

Brandon- Oh Mom, can we stay a little longer?

Sasha- Yes Mom, can we?

Kim- Sorry but we have to go, I have to go and prepare dinner.

Teddy- Why do you have to take my grandkids away from me?

Kim- Dad, stop being ridiculous.

Teddy- You heard the kids, they want to stay.

Kim- I am sorry but we have to go. You can see your grandkids anytime, you know where we live. Let's go; kids, kiss your grandparents bye.

Sasha and Brandon walk over to Teddy.

Sasha- (Hugs him) Bye Grandpa.

Teddy- Never say bye, say see you later, okay.

Sasha- Okay, see you later Grandpa.

Teddy- Love you, Precious.

Brandon- Take care, Grandpa.

Teddy- I don't know when I am going to see you all again.

Kim- Dad, just stop it.

Teddy- Stop what? We only see our grandkids once a month if we are lucky.

Kim- That is ridiculous and I am not going to stay here and argue over this.

Stephanie- He is right.

Kim- Well you know where we live, you can come and see them anytime.

Teddy- Why should we have to always come to your house to see our grandkids? They should come and visit us and spend time with us.

Kim- The last time I checked you both drive, so I do not see the problem. (she turns to Kevin) See you Kevin, it was good seeing you.

Kevin- You too. Tell Michael I said hello.

Kim- I will.

The kids run over to Kevin and hug him.

Sasha- See you later Uncle Kevin.

Kevin- (kisses her on the cheeks) Take care.

Brandon- (hugs Kevin) See you later Uncle Kevin.

Kevin- Take care big guy.

> Kim and the kids leave. Stephanie and Kevin are
> in the kitchen

Stephanie- Son, is everything okay?

Kevin- Yes Mom, everything is fine.

Stephanie- You know that you can tell me anything and I will still love you.

Kevin- (smiles) I know that, Mom. Look I have to head out for rehearsals. I will call you later.

Stephanie- Have a good show, Son. I love you.

Kevin- Thanks, Mom. I love you more.

> Stephanie walks over and hugs Kevin.

Stephanie- It was so good seeing you, you are still my Baby.

Kevin- I know that, Mom.

Stephanie- I will always be here for you.

Kevin- I know that, Mom.

> They are still hugging.

Stephanie- I wish you would stay here as opposed to the hotel.

Kevin- Mom, you know it would not work out.

Stephanie- Why not?

Kevin- Mom, let's not get into it.

Stephanie- You know Kevin, your dad is a changed man.

Kevin- Is he now?

Stephanie- If you would sit down and talk with him you will know.

Kevin- Dad and I sitting down and talking? That would be a first.

Stephanie- Oh Kevin.

Kevin- Mom, its okay. I really have to get going.

Stephanie- Okay Son, I will walk you out.

Kevin- You really do not have to.

Stephanie- I know but I want to.

> Kevin walks into the living room to say good-bye to his dad, and Teddy is watching the game.

Kevin- Oh well, I am heading out.

Teddy- (turns around to Kevin) Okay have a good trip. Play well tonight.

Kevin- Thanks.

> Teddy turns back around and continues to watch the game, Kevin stands and look at him for a few minutes and then he makes his way to the front door, Stephanie walks behind him. He opens the door and turns to hug his mom again.

Kevin- It was good seeing you.

Stephanie- (hugs him) I wish I saw you often. Play well tonight. I love you.

Kevin- Love you too, see ya.

Stephanie- Call me when you get to the hotel.

Kevin- I will.

> Stephanie stands at the door as Kevin walks to his Range Rover. He gets in and waves good-bye, Stephanie waves back to him. Stephanie walks into the living room where Teddy is still watching the game.

Stephanie- (turns to Teddy and asks) Wasn't it good seeing Kevin?

Teddy- Yeah.

Stephanie- You barely said two words to him.

Teddy- Stephanie please, Kevin does not have anything to say to me, and I certainly do not have anything to say to him, either.

Stephanie- You just treat him like a stepchild.

Teddy- (annoyed) What the hell are you talking about? Kevin is a grown man, if he wanted to talk to me he could have. I do not want to discuss this anymore. I am watching a game.

Stephanie- Why do you hate him, Teddy?

> Teddy does not answer.

Stephanie- I said why do you hate your own son?

Teddy- (upset) What the hell are you talking about? How dare you accuse me of this? I am warning you Woman, I do not want to have this conversation.

> Stephanie walks out of the room.

Scene 5

Michael is at home in the kitchen preparing dinner for his wife and family, the phones rings.

Michael- Hello.

Stephanie- Is Kim there?

Michael- (shaking his head in disbelief) Well hello Mrs. Tucker, how are you?

Stephanie- I asked if my daughter and kids are at home?

Michael- No, Kim and the kids are not home yet.

Stephanie- Hmm that's odd, they left here over an hour ago, it only takes 45 minutes from our house to yours. Are you sure they are not there?

Michael- No they are not. I will have Kim call you when she gets home.

Teddy is in the background yelling.

Teddy- They are not home yet? How come?

Stephanie- You had better not be lying to me, I swear.

Michael- (raising his voice) Mrs. Tucker please, stop with the swearing. Your daughter is not here. I will have her call you when she gets home. Have a nice evening.

Stephanie- (holding the phone in her hands in disbelief) That fool hung up on me.

Teddy- (shocked) He did what?

Stephanie- Michael hung up the phone on me, can you believe that?

Teddy- Hell no. Give me that phone.

> Teddy gets up and grabs the phone from his wife
> and hits the redial button.

Stephanie- Honey, what are you doing?

Teddy- What does it look like I am doing, I am calling Michael, he owes you an apology.

> Michael looks at the caller id and does not an-
> swer. The voice mail comes on and Teddy leaves
> a message.

Teddy- Michael you son of a bitch, you hung up on my wife, how dare you? You had better call her right back and apologize. What kind of a man are you?

> Michael listens to the message then deletes it. He
> walks back to the oven to check on the steak.
> Kim and the kids pulls up in the driveway, Kim's
> nosey neighbor Paula is doing her usual peeking.

Paula- Hmm, if it isn't the single mom and her kids.

Raymond- Paula for the life of God, can you stop spying on those folks? What have they done to you?

Paula- They act like they are better than everyone else. She acts like she has the perfect marriage and I can smell trouble.

Raymond- (shaking his head) You need to worry about what is going on in your own marriage.

Paula- It's apparent nothing is happening.

Raymond- I am getting so tired of your smart ass comments.

Paula- And I am tired of you.

Raymond- Keep that up, keep talking trash to me.

Paula- Is that a threat? Negro, please.

    She continues to look out the window.

Raymond- (talking to himself) Okay, we will see who has the last laugh.

Paula- Stop mumbling to yourself, if you have something to say, say it to my face. If you want out of this marriage or whatever just let me now.

    Raymond walks out of the room.
    Kim and the kids walk to their front door, as she
    opens the door she can smell the aroma.

Kim- Hmm, something smells good.

Brandon- Yeah real good, someone has been cooking.

    They all walk into the kitchen and there is Michael setting the table.

Kim- (surprised) Honey, are you cooking?

Michael- (turns around and smiles) Yes, your dinner is ready. Please wash your hands and have a seat. Oh, by the way Kim, your parents called.

Kim- What's the occasion?

Michael- There is no occasion; I just wanted to cook dinner for my family.

Kim- (walks over and kisses him) I love you.

Sasha- Oh boy here we go again.

Michael, Kim and Brandon all laugh.

Michael- Okay, you all go and wash your hands and let's get ready to eat.

Kim- What did you cook?

Michael- Honey, just sit down and let me cater to you and the kids.

Everyone sits at the table, Kim blesses the food.

Brandon- Okay, let's eat.

Michael- Honey, how was church?

Kim- It was okay.

Michael- Just okay?

Kim- Well it was crowded as usual, everyone kept asking about you.

Brandon- Yeah, folks were being Nosey as usual.

Michael- Sounds like the usual.

Kim- Yep. How was your day?

Michael- It was good; Malik and I had a great workout.

Kim- That's great, how are things going with him and Karen?

Michael- Not good.

Kim- I am sorry to hear that, they make such a great couple.

Michael- Yes they sure do.

Sasha- Dad, this food is delicious.

Brandon- Yes Dad, you should cook Sunday dinner more often.

Kim- Oh what are you all trying to say, you all do not like my cooking?

Sasha- No Mom, we love your cooking, but Dad is a little better.

Brandon- Yes just a little.

Kim Looks at Michael and they both smile.

Brandon- I thought you were going to the office to work on that case.

Michael- Yeah that was my plan but I decided to spend some quality time with my family.

Sasha- You are such a great dad.

Brandon- Thanks Dad, dinner was delicious. (he gets up and put his dish in the sink)

Michael- Good to hear.

Sasha- Yeah Dad, it really was. (she also gets up from the table and puts her dish in the sink, she walks over and kisses him on the cheeks)

Kim- You all go up stairs and get cleaned up.

Brandon & Sasha- Okay, Mom.

Kim- (looks at Michael) Honey, dinner was delicious. I love you so much.

Michael- Thanks, Honey. I love you more.

> Kim reaches over and kisses him. After kissing
> they both get up and clean up the table; Michael
> puts the dishes in the sink and Kim washes the
> dishes.

Kim- Okay, the dishes are done. Let's go to bed. I am tired.

Michael- I will check on the kids.

> Kim is lying in bed; Michael walks in.

Michael- Okay, the kids are in bed.

Kim- Good. Honey I have some good news and bad news.

Michael- What's up? Tell me the good news first.

Kim- Well you know that "Casual Attire" won the fashion show
and I have to go Paris to promote the clothing line.

Michael- Yes you told me. I think that is great. I am so proud
of you.

Kim- Well, the bad news is I have to go Paris in two weeks.

Michael- Okay, what date?

> Kim looks at Michael and says nothing.

Michael- What date Kim?

Kim- (mumbles) June 17th.

Michael- What did you say? I could not hear you. What date?

Kim- June 17th.

Michael- Kim! That is our anniversary, how could you? We
made plans.

Kim- I am so sorry, Honey. I told them that, but the date has been set and I have to go. I don't want to but I have to.

Michael- Excuse me! You have to go? You don't have to do a damn thing.

Kim- Yes, Michael. If I don't go I could get sued, that was part of wining the contract; that I would go to Paris and promote my clothing line. I just can't back out on them. I worked really hard for this, Honey.

Michael- I understand that, but if the shoe were on the other foot Kim, you would be livid, and you know it.

Kim- Probably, but I would understand and would be supportive.

Michael- Oh what, I am not supportive? Is that what you are saying?

Kim- Yes, that is exactly what I am saying.

Michael- I can't believe you just uttered those words. All I have ever been was supportive, and this is the thanks I get. You know what, I am not even going to go there. Good night, Kim.

Kim- No, let's go there.

Michael- Look it's late and the kids are asleep, let's not argue.

Kim- You know Michael, sometimes I think you are jealous of me and my success.

Michael- (sits up on the bed) What? That is ridiculous and you know it.

Kim- No, I am serious. When I was a full time stay at home mom you loved it; you loved being the breadwinner. You loved bringing home the bacon.

Michael- I'm still the breadwinner, so what is your point? Don't act like you did not enjoy it? Like going to the spa with your friends, getting a nanny to watch the kids while you got a personal trainer and went on shopping sprees. You even hired a chef and a maid. It's not like you stayed home and cooked and cleaned. So you loved it, so don't even try to complain now.

Kim- That is not the point.

Michael- Then what is your point?

Kim- When I told you I wanted to open my boutique, you thought I was crazy.

Michael- Was I wrong? You had no idea about running a boutique; you just like the fact of owning one. But as usual, being the SUPPORTIVE husband, I said sure, if that is what you want then do it. Whatever you wanted to do I have supported. I am so sick and tired of you saying that shit to me, Kim. I don't deserve it.

Kim- (gets quiet) Well, you make me say that sometimes.

Michael- What? That does not make any sense to me, you are just spoiled. Maybe I am part to blame for that. I should stop giving you whatever you need.

Sasha- (hears the argument coming from her parent's room, gets up and runs over to Brandon's room. She begins whispering as she shakes Brandon) Brandon, Brandon! Wake up.

Brandon- (rubbing his eyes, half awake) Sasha is that you?

Sasha- (whispering) Yes, wake up.

Brandon- What are you doing in my room? Did you have a nightmare?

Sasha- (whispering) No.

Brandon- Then why are you here? And why are you whispering?

Sasha- Ssssh, listen.

Brandon- Listen to what? Sasha, not again, if Mom and Dad are making noise again let them; we are not going in their room to find out anything.

Sasha- No you stupid, listen.

Brandon- Listen to what, do you have your TV on?

Sasha- No silly it's Mom and Dad, they are arguing.

Brandon- That is what couples do, Sasha.

Sasha- It is really bad, they have been arguing for over twenty minutes.

Brandon- How do you know that?

Sasha- Because I have been timing it. We need to do something. I do not want them to argue and end up getting a divorce.

Brandon- That is not going to happen, go back to your room.

Sasha- (begins to cry) They are going to get a divorce, I don't want to be without a mom and a dad. (she cries even harder).

Brandon- (gets up and hugs Sasha) That is never going to happen to Mom and Dad, they love each other.

Sasha- Then why won't they stop arguing? We need to do something.

Brandon- No, we need to mind our business and let grown folks take care of their issues.

Sasha- If you don't do something, I will.

Brandon- And what are you going to do?

Sasha- I am going to walk in the room and tell them to stop.

Brandon- Sasha, that is not a good idea.

Sasha- Well, do you have a better one?

Brandon- No, I am going back to bed, and I suggest you do the same.

Sasha- No.

Brandon- Okay, let's wait awhile; let's give them fifteen minutes and if they are still arguing then I will think of something.

Sasha- Okay.

Brandon- (looks at his clock) Okay, its 9:00 pm. If they do not stop arguing by 9:15 pm we will do something.

Sasha- What are you going to do?

Brandon- I do not know.

Sasha- It's 9:20 pm and they are still arguing. Now what?

Brandon- I don't know, Sasha. What do you want me to do?

Sasha- Make them stop.

Brandon- I can't.

Sasha- (begins to scream very loud) AAAAAH! AAAAAAAAAAAAAAAAAAH!

Brandon- What are you doing?

Sasha- Distracting them.

Brandon- Stop that right now before you get in trouble.

Sasha- I don't care.

> Sasha screams out again even louder
> AAAAAAAAAAAAAAAAAAAAAAH
> AAAAAAAAAAAAAAAAHH!

Brandon- Have you lost your mind?

Sasha- Maybe.

Kim- (says to Michael) Did you hear that?

Michael- Yeah, it sounds like Sasha.

> Michael and Kim both run over to Sasha's room, before they get there, they see the lights on in Brandon's room and stops there first.

Michael- What the hell is going on?

Kim- Is everything okay?

Brandon- Well Sasha, go ahead and tell Mom.

Kim- Tell me what?

Michael- This had better be good.

Sasha- (stuttering and talking slow) Am, well ah.

Michael- We are waiting.

Sasha- Well I heard you all arguing, you all were arguing for half an hour and I was scared and could not sleep.

Kim- Why are you in Brandon's room?

Sasha- Well I came to Brandon.

Michael- For what?

Sasha- To see if he could make you all stop arguing, I was scared.

Kim- Scared of what?

Sasha- Scared that you all were going to argue and get a divorce.

Kim- Sasha, how many times do I have to tell you that couples argue sometimes? It does not mean that they will get a divorce. And it's not your job to make anyone stop arguing. Please promise me you will not do that again.

Michael- Yes, you had us both scared.

Sasha- See, that is exactly how I felt when I heard you all arguing, I was scared. Please do not argue anymore.

Kim- Sasha Sweetie, we cannot promise that. We will try to keep our voices down, but we are going to have our disagreements sometimes.

Brandon- See, I told you.

Michael- Okay, let's all go back to bed.

Sasha- Sorry Mom and Dad.

Brandon- What about me?

Sasha- Sorry, Brandon.

> Michael and Kim leave the room; Sasha goes
> back to her room.

Kim- Can you believe that?

Michael- Maybe we just need to keep our voices down.

Kim- I agree, but she cannot be screaming out like that whenever we argue.

Michael- Yes, you are right. Let's get some sleep; we can discuss this stuff tomorrow.

Kim- Let's just finish it off, let me just say before I get your support, I have to go through a whole lot of interrogations. Michael I hate when you do that; I feel like one of your clients, not your wife.

Michael- That is all in your head.

Kim- No its not, you do it all the time and I am sick and tired of it.

Michael- What else are you sick and tired of Kim? You might as well get it all out now.

Kim- Fine. I am sick and tired of you missing dinner with me and the kids; I am sick and tired of you bringing your work home all the time; I am sick and tired of you not going to church with me and the kids; and I am sick and tired of you making me feel like a trophy wife. I am smart and I have skills. I am sick and tired of being sick and tired. (Kim's voice breaks and she begins to cry)

Michael- (reaches over to her and hugs her saying) Baby, I never knew you felt this way. I wish you had told me.

Kim- (crying) I have told you, you just never listened.

Michael- Baby, I am sorry. I love you and all I ever wanted was to make you happy and be a good husband. I will start going back to church with you and the kids as soon as this case blows over. I have never treated you like trophy wife. About me bringing my work home, I do that in order to be here with you and the kids, if not I will have to be at the office during the weekends and weekdays. I have tried to have dinner with you and the kids as much as possible, but sometimes I just can't, and I need you to understand that. (Michael wipes her tears away with his hands saying) Look at me.

Kim looks at Michael.

Michael- I love you very much and all I want to do is make you happy, if you are sad I'm sad.

Kim- I'm sorry; I did not mean to go off in a tangent like that, but sometimes I just feel that you are not supportive. Look. I am going to call the agency tomorrow and explain that I will not be able to make the trip.

Michael- No, I do not want you to do that.

Kim- Are you sure?

Michael- Yes. I know how much this means to you; we will just compromise and celebrate our anniversary early that's all.

Kim- (excited, hugs Michael) Oh Michael. Thank you, Honey. I really do appreciate that. I promise I will make it up to you.

Michael- Well, you know I am good old supportive Michael.

They both laugh.

Kim- So what did you have in mind?

Michael- I was thinking of throwing a party just for family and close friends. I mean we have done the traveling thing so this would be different.

Kim- That is a fabulous idea.

Michael- Good, let's get some sleep. I have a long day tomorrow.

Kim- Lets have make up sex.

Michael- No Kim, I think we had enough interruptions with the kids tonight.

Kim- I promise I will not be vocal.

Michael- Nope, remember we are having lunch tomorrow. I will take care of you then.

Kim- (smiles and says) You are so naughty and I love it.

She reaches over to kiss him goodnight.

Kim- Good night.

Scene 6

Michael is driving in his silver Bugatti Veyron. He pulls up to his parking spot marked reserved for MJS CEO Stevenson & Stevenson LLP. He parks his car, grabs his briefcase and walks to the elevator. As he gets to the elevator there are two other employees waiting there.

Tosha- (in a flirtatious tone) Good morning Mr. Stevenson, how are you this morning?

Michael- Good morning Tosha, I am fine and you?

Tosha- I'm a bit tired but after my coffee I will be fine.

Michael- That's good.

Natalie- Mr. Stevenson, that is a bad suit.

Tosha- Yes that is tight.

Michael- Thank you.

Tosha- (gets off on the seventh) Have a blessed day everyone.

Michael & Natalie- (says) You too.

Natalie- (gets off on the eight floor) Take care Mr. Stevenson.

Michael- Take care.

> Michael's firm owns the 7th floor to the 12th floor, all the executives are on the twelfth floor, Michael gets off the elevator and walks by the reception desk.

Wendy- (with a bubbly attitude) Good morning Mr. Stevenson, that is such a nice suit.

Michael- Good morning, thanks Wendy. I have to credit my wife for this.

Wendy- Well it is obvious she has good taste. (she gives him a flirtatious look)

> Wendy looks him up and down as if she wanted to eat him up, as Michael walks toward his office, three other co-workers are whispering to each other about him.

Co-worker #1- Damn, he is fine. His wife is so damn lucky.

Co- worker #2- Lucky is an understatement.

Co-worker #3- All I want is one hour with him, just one hour.

> Co-worker #1 & co-worker #2 laugh.

Co-worker #2- Pick a number and get in line.

> They all laugh and walk back to their cubicles, as Michael gets closer. Michael passes by his Executive Assistant Secretary Nicole

Nicole- Good morning, Mr. Stevenson.

Michael- Good Morning, Nicole.

> Michael walks into his office, his office over-
> looks the city, and the view is spectacular. He
> puts his briefcase on his desk and before he could
> do anything else, Nicole walks in his office. His
> office is open, however, she knocks on the door.

Nicole- Can I get you some coffee before I brief you on your
day?

Michael- No coffee, let's discuss the schedule.

> Nicole sits down in the chair in front of Michael,
> she crosses her legs very slowly, and Michael is
> not moved.

Nicole- How was your weekend?

Michael- It was great, thanks for asking. And yours?

Nicole- Well my girlfriends and I went out to dinner on Satur-
day. Sunday I treated myself to a pedicure and manicure.

Michael- Oh that is great.

> Nicole looks at her notes and gives Michael a
> breakdown of his day.

Nicole- Okay at 9:00 a.m., which is in half an hour, you have a
visit with Mr. Snyder, 10:30 a.m. you have the Manager's
meeting. 12:00 o'clock is lunch with Judge Zelwiegburg. 2:00
p.m. you have a conference call. At 4:00 p.m. a meeting with the
CFO and COO. That meeting is scheduled to end at 7:00; looks
like you will be working late tonight and missing dinner with
your family.

Michael- Yes it seems that way, which is unfortunate.

Nicole- (stammers) Since I am working late too, maybe we can grab a bite to eat together.

Michael- Thanks Nicole, but no thanks.

Nicole- (feels rejected) Okay. Have a great day.

> Nicole leaves Michael's office. A client of his is on her way up to see him; the client stops at Nicole's desk.

Ms. Tegenes- Nicole good morning, where is Michael?

Nicole- Ms. Tegenes, you do not have an appointment.

Ms.Tegenes- I don't need an appointment, are you going to tell him I'm here or what?

Nicole- (Stammers) Wait, just wait.

> Nicole runs into Michael's office.

Nicole- Sorry Michael but Ms. Tegenes is here, she does not have an appointment but she wants to see you.

Michael- (sighs) Just send her in. Thanks Nicole.

> Ms. Tegenes walks in Michael's office and she stands at the door with her hands on her hips, she is wearing a very short leopard black and brown dress with a very low V neck, her boobs are about a 40 D, and she is wearing matching leopard six inch heels.

Michael- (looks at her and shakes his head) Come on in Ms. Tegenes. What can I do for you today?

Ms. Teneges- (closes the door) How many times do I need to tell you, just call me Janet. Call me Janet if you're nasty. (she laughs)

Michael- Ms. Teneges I do not have time for you and your games, my time is very limited, especially since you do not have an appointment. What can I do for you?

Ms. Tegenes- I thought you would never ask. Well for starters you can give me a nice tight hug.

Michael- (annoyed) Ms. Tegenes, What is it?

Ms. Teneges- You know, I am starting to wonder about you. Are you gay or something? Because all the advances I've thrown at you and you keep ignoring me; it's just not normal. You know, it makes me wonder.

Michael- Ms. Teneges, I am a happily married man, and trust me I am not interested. Like I said earlier, what can I do for you?

Ms. Teneges- You need to stop playing hard to get. I've heard that saying before that I'm happily married. Please, that does not move me.

Michael- If you do not state why you are here I will have to ask you to leave. Again, what can I do for you?

Ms. Teneges- (talking in a seductive voice) There is a lot that you can do for me, but I am not sure if you can handle it. (she touches her breasts) But for starters I need more alimony money. What I am receiving is not enough to cover my expenses; I mean my kids' expenses.

Michael- No you said it right at first, you mean your other expenses Ms. Teneges

Ms. Teneges- I said to call me Janet.

Michael- I don't have time for you today Ms. Teneges. If you need more money I cannot help you, so what else can I assist you with?

Ms. Teneges- I said call me Janet. Call me Janet if you are nasty.

Michael- (annoyed he yells) Janet, I want you out of my office.

Ms. Teneges- See Baby, that just rolls off of your tongue so smoothly, I wonder what else rolls off of your tongue that easily.

Michael- (ignores her comments) The money you received is not for face lifts, tummy tucks, lipo or things of that nature, it's for you and your kids.

Ms. Teneges- (upset) How dare you! Are you accusing me of using the money for that? What you see here (she begins touching her body) is all pure, Baby. I have not had a tummy tuck or lipo, yes I am 50 years old, but I look like I am 30, so don't hate. I want more money.

Michael- I'm afraid that I would not be able to assist you with that.

Ms. Tegenes- (walks closer to Michael, and says) I was married to that bastard for 20 years. He cheated on me for 18 of those years. Now $20,000 a month is just not enough. I need more, I deserve more.

Michael- (yelling) Ms. Teneges, sit down.

Ms. Teneges- (getting loud) I said to call me Janet. What, you don't like me getting that close to you? What, it turns you on?

> She gets even closer, she pulls the zipper at the
> back of her dress, the dress falls to the ground
> and she is butt naked.

Michael- (disgusted) Ms. Teneges, what the hell are you doing?

Ms. Teneges- What does it look like, big guy?

> She then jumps on Michael and wrap her legs around him, Michael quickly throws her off of him, he throws her so hard that she flies to the other end of the floor, the same time Nicole walks in the office she sees Ms. Teneges on the floor half naked, Nicole closes the door quickly.

Michael- (talking to Ms. Teneges) You have two seconds to get dressed and get the hell out of my office, and if you ever, ever step foot back into this building I will personally throw you out and have you arrested. (Michael raises his voice) Do you hear me?

> Ms. Teneges is on the floor in shock; she is a bit shaken up.

Ms. Teneges- (scared) Sure, whatever you say Michael, but you made the worst mistake by putting your hands on me; you will pay for this, you bastard.

Michael- (yelling) Get out! Get out now! And don't you ever return here.

> Ms. Teneges tries to put on her clothes quickly, but Michael throws her out of his office, which is not too far from where Nicole sits. Nicole is embarrassed and she gives Ms. Teneges a coat to cover herself.

Nicole- (concerned) Are you okay?

Ms. Teneges- (rudely responds) Do I look okay to you? Where is the bathroom?

Nicole- I was just trying to help, I will take you there.

Ms. Teneges- Yes, do that.

> Nicole walks her to the ladies room, as she passes
> by cubicles, employees are looking on in shock,
> trying to find out what is going on.

Ms. Teneges- What the hell are you all looking at, don't you all
have work to do?

Nicole- Here is the bathroom.

> Ms. Teneges walks in; Nicole slowly walks into
> Michael office and asks,

Nicole- Mr. Stevenson are you okay?

Michael- (he pauses for five seconds and then response) Yes
Nicole I am fine. If Ms. Teneges ever steps foot in this building
again, have her arrested.

Nicole- Will do sir. Don't forget your next appointment is in ten
minutes.

Michael- Thanks Nicole.

> Ms. Teneges is in the bathroom, she throws cold
> water on her face and begins to walk out of the
> bathroom.

Scene 7

Kim is at her boutique going through her phone book inviting everyone to her ten year anniversary party; the first person she calls is her brother James. James lives in Rochester New York with his wife and three boys. James is a doctor. Kim dials his home.

Kelly- Hello.

Kim- Kelly?

Kelly- Yes this is Kelly

Kim- Kelly how are you doing? It's Kim.

Kelly- Well hello Kim, how are you doing?

Kim- I am doing great, thanks for asking.

Kelly- How is the family?

Kim- We are doing great, just great, what about you?

Kelly- Everything is great, I have no complaints.

Kim- How are my nephews doing? I bet they have grown so tall since the last time I saw them.

Kelly- (laughs) Big is an understatement. Christopher is 5'6" and he is only eleven, but that is our future basketball player. Christian plays soccer now and he is so good at it, and our little one Collin is just a bundle of joy. He is into everything; he is five going on twenty.

> They both laugh.

Kim- That is so sweet, glad to know that they are doing fine. The reason for my call is Michael and I will be celebrating our ten year anniversary in two weeks, I know it's short notice but hopefully you and my brother can attend. It's going to be held at our home.

Kelly- Consider me there, as for James I'm not sure, he is always on call so I could not say.

Kim- I know, someone has to save lives right? But let him know that I called and it would mean a lot to me if he could make it, if not I would understand.

Kelly- Knowing your brother, he is going to do everything he can to be there.

Kim- Great, well take care Kelly, kiss the boys for me and see you all in two weeks.

Kelly- Okay Kim, see you then, thanks for calling.

Kim- Anytime, take care.

Kelly- Bye.

> Kim hangs up the phone and continues to call her family and friends; a customer walks into her store, then another, then another. Kim gets off the phone and walks over to greet them.

Kim- Hello how are you all doing? Can I assist you in finding something?

Customer #1- I am just looking, thank you.

Customer #2- (friendly) I am looking for the silk pedal pushers.

Kim- I have a few left in the back on the left hand side, let me know if you need further assistance.

Customer #2- Thank you very much.

Customer #3- (rudely) I don't need any help, thanks. (and walks away from Kim)

Kim- Okay, but if you need me I will be right here.

Customer #3 rolls her eyes and keeps on walking.

Customer #1- (Picks up two pairs of jeans and walks toward Kim to checkout) I would love to pay for these please.

Kim- These are such great jeans, great choice. Are both pairs for you or someone else?

Customer #1- (in a friendly tone) One is for me and the other is for my sister.

Kim- That is great, you are going to love them. Your total is $85.96, will it be cash or charge?

Customer #1- Charge please.

Kim rings up the merchandise.

Kim- Thank you Mrs. Stein, have a great day.

Customer #1- (smiles) Take care.

Customer #2- (walks up to Kim) Can I try these on?

Kim- Sure, the fitting room is over to your left and the doors are open.

Customer #2- Great, thanks.

> Kim gets back on the phone and continues to call friends and family, as she leaves a message for one of her girlfriend, she sees that Customer #3 is doing something suspicious; Kim quickly gets off the phone and walks over to her.

Kim- Are you finding everything okay?

Customer #3- (with attitude) Yes, if I need your assistance I will let you know.

> As Kim walks away she notices that the customer's bag is bulkier than when she came in. Kim is unsure how to approach the customer, she walks closer to get a better look as to what is in her bag, she sees fabric sticking out of the bag but not sure if it's from her store. She begins talking to the customer.

Kim- Those tops that you are admiring are buy one get one free.

Customer #3- That's good to know, but I really do not see anything that I need out of this store, thanks for your assistance.

> The customer walks out but as she walks out of the store, the security beeper goes off, the customer is shocked and tries to play it off, and Kim comes rushing to assist.

Customer #3- I am not sure why that went off, it must be my diamond earrings.

Kim- Yes probably, however, I need to check your bag.

Customer #3- (annoyed) I beg your pardon? You need to check my bag?

Kim- Yes, I need to check your bag.

Customer #3- (upset) Are you accusing me of stealing? Because I can buy this entire store if I wanted to.

Kim- I am not accusing you of anything, 10 times out of 10 when that buzzer goes off it's because there is a sensor on the clothing.

Customer #3- But I did not purchase anything from this store, maybe it's the lipstick I bought from Saks.

Kim- Ma'am, please open your bag.

Customer #3- No! Do you know who I am?

Kim- No and I don't care to know.

Customer #3- I am Mrs. Kolevgic wife of Ambassador Kolevigjc; I can have you arrested with one phone call.

Kim- I am not going to ask you again to show me your purse, Ma'am.

Customer #3- You are a nobody. (she begins to walk out of the store) Kim grabs her bag and throws her to the floor.

Customer #3- (screaming) How dare you?

Kim- Shut up, you are stealing from me. (Kim looks into the bag and sees two of her silk shirts worth $100)

Customer #3- I will have you fired tomorrow, I am sure the owner just put a black face to promote diversity, but one phone call and you will be fired.

Kim- I am the owner and you stole two lace tops from me both totaling $100. You have three options, pay for the tops, leave them here or face charges for shoplifting, what is it going to be Mrs. Kolevigic?

Customer #3- (gets up and dusts off her clothing) You bitch, you just made the worst mistake ever. How dare you put your hands on me?

> She reaches in her bag pulls out the two lace tops
> and throws them on the floor saying

Customer #3- You can have your cheap tops, Saks has a better quality of them.

Kim- Get out.

Customer #3- You have no idea how much power I have.

Kim- Get out, I really do not care.

> Kim picks up the blouses off the floor and walks
> back to the counter.

Customer #2- I am going to pass, they are too tight. I will try back in two weeks; by that time I should have lost some pounds

Kim- Okay, have a great day.

> Kim looks at her watch its 2:30 pm she is won-
> dering where her part time clerk is, before she di-
> als her number, the clerk comes running in.

Clerk- Hello Mrs. Stevenson, sorry I am late, but there was a terrible accident on the freeway.

Kim- Hello Tammy, oh it's not a problem. Oh by the way Tammy, we just had someone trying to shoplift some clothing.

Tammy- I don't understand why folks do that.

Kim- Me neither. Okay I have to run and pick up my kids. If you need me just call my cell.

Clerk- Okay enjoy your day.

Kim- Bye.

> Kim gets into her car and drives to the kids'
> school, there is a lot of traffic and she worries she
> will be late and have to pay a late charge. Her
> phone rings, it's Michael.

Kim- Hey, Honey.

Michael- How are you?

Kim- Just fine, on my way to pick up the kids. Are you going to
be home for dinner?

Michael- I doubt it, we are all still here working on this case.

Kim- (disappointed) Oh okay, we are having leftovers anyway.
What time do you think you will be home?

Michael- Maybe around 9-9:30 pm.

Kim- Okay, see you when you get home.

Scene 8

It's the next morning and Kim is putting on her jeans and tee shirt, Michael is brushing his teeth. She walks over to Michael who is in the bathroom and says,

Kim- Are you taking the kids out for breakfast or are you making breakfast?

Michael- I think I will take them out.

Kim- Sounds like a good idea. Okay so you know I am going to the spa and then this evening is Girls' night out.

Michael- Yes, I know that and me and the kids have our own plans.

Kim- Oh okay, well try not to miss me.

Michael- You know I will.

> Kim's cell phone rings it's Sharon. Sharon recently ended a 13-year marriage, and it was a nasty divorce to say the least and she is very bitter. Kim answers.

Kim- Hey, Girl.

Sharon- Where are you? I am pulling up at the spa.

Kim- I am en route, I will be there in twenty minutes. How are you doing?

Sharon- Right now I am doing great because I am spending all of that bastard's money. I am getting everything today. Facial, pedicure, manicure, and massage.

Kim- Where are the kids?

Sharon- The kids are spending the weekend with that mother-fucker and his new bitch.

Kim- Sharon! Sharon let's try not to curse when talking about Derrick, okay.

Sharon- Do me a favor, do not mention that bastard's name, just say my ex or D.

Kim- Fine.

Sharon- So how is the family?

Kim- The family is great thanks for asking. Have you called the others and reminded them of Girls' night out?

Sharon-Yep I did and we are all set.

Kim- Good. Are you coming?

Sharon- Of course, you know there is always some drama or mess going on. I am always down for the madness.

Kim- (laughing) You are crazy. I am glad everyone is coming, especially, Monisha.

Sharon- I am not sure about her.

Kim- I thought you said we were set.

Sharon- I spoke to everyone and they said yes. I left Monisha a message. She probably will not come, you know since she got engaged she does not have time for her friends; it's all about Mark.

Kim- Yeah I know, I told her to try to come out for some air and give the brother some space.

Sharon- Alright, hurry up and get here.

Kim- Okay bye see you shortly.

> Kim hangs up and begins to dial Monisha's cell. Her voice mail comes on so Kim leaves a message.

Kim- Mo, call me when you get a chance.

> Kim then calls Monisha's house and the voice mail comes on. She does not leave a message. Kim's cell phones rings.

Kim- Hello.

James- Hey there, Little Sis.

Kim- (excited) James how are you doing? I am so glad to hear from you.

James- I am doing great, so you are having a party, ha?

Kim- Yes and tell me that you will be there?

James- Of course I would not miss it for the world.

Kim- How is work?

James- Busy as usual.

Kim- You are the best doctor that hospital has.

Kim- Thanks, Sis.

James- How are Michael and the kids?

Kim- We are doing great; the kids are fine.

James- Wow! It's been two years since I've seen you.

Kim- I know.

> Kim hears in the background paging Dr. James
> Tucker, please report to the emergency room.

James- (talking really fast) Hey, I have to go I am being paged.

Kim- I know, I can hear it in the background. See you next week.

James- I would not miss it for the world.

Kim- Love you.

James- Love you, too.

Kim- Bye.

Scene 9

Raymond and Paula are Kim's next door neighbors. Raymond and Paula are lying in bed. Raymond reaches over to Paula and tries to arouse her.

Paula- (disgusted moves away from him) What the hell are you doing?

Raymond- (annoyed) I am trying to make love to my wife, is that a crime?

Paula- Well it's not working so stop.

Raymond- You know a man has needs.

Paula- And?

Raymond- And I need my wife to want me.

Paula- I am just not in the mood, I am tired. We hardly make love Raymond so why are you acting like we have an active sex life?

Raymond- Who's fault is that?

Paula- Who the hell knows and who cares?

Raymond- You are the kind of wife that will make your man cheat.

Paula- Do what you have to do.

Raymond reaches out to her again.

Paula- (pulls herself away saying) Stop Raymond, I am not in the mood.

Raymond- You are never in the fucking mood, I am getting tired of this shit; I ain't going to beg my own wife for sex.

Paula- (getting out of the bed) Then don't.

Raymond- You would rather peek at the Stevensons all day than take care of your man, but you know that is all good, because what you are not willing to do, someone else will.

Paula- Does it look like I am bothered? You just got a lot of talk and no action. That is the problem. That is what our marriage is right now, no action.

Paula goes into the bathroom to take a shower.
She gets in the shower and turns it on.

Raymond- (walks into the bathroom) Don't take forever in the damn shower either. I have somewhere to go.

Paula- You will just have to wait until I'm done, however long that takes.

Raymond- I am so sick and tired of you and that smart ass mouth.

Paula- Get over it.

Raymond- (looks at his fist) You know Paula, you are the kind of woman that wants a man to beat you, you really are. But you know what, I ain't going to jail for no woman. You are not worth it. See, you do not appreciate a good man who communicates to you nicely; you want a man who talks to you with his fists. You like to provoke a man, break a man down, and I am so tired of you and that shit. I have tried, and tried, for six mother-fucking years, putting up with your bullshit and smart mouth, but no more Paula, no motherfucking more.

Paula- Are you finished now? Because I need to take a shower, I have a busy day ahead of me.

> Raymond walks out of the bathroom, shaking his head.

Paula- (says) Punk ass bitch.

> Raymond hears it and goes back in the bathroom, he pulls the curtains.

Paula- (covers her body with her hands) What the hell are you doing? I am taking a shower.

Raymond- What did you just call me?

Paula- I said you punk ass bitch, and I did not stutter.

Raymond- (pauses for ten seconds) You know what, you want me to put my hands on you, you want a man to kick your ass and then get locked up, but I am bigger than that, you keep that shit up Paula; keep it up, you are going to get what's coming to you.

Paula- Is that a threat? Please go ahead and make my day. I dare you.

> Raymond walks out of the bathroom, the phone rings and he answers.

Raymond- Hello.

Male Caller- Is Paula there?

Raymond- Who the fuck is this?

Male Caller- Man, is she there? I do not need to answer to you, who the fuck are you?

Raymond- (angry) I am her husband.

Male Caller- (shocked) I'm Calvin and she told me she was single. Man these bitches out here are so damn crazy.

Raymond- Oh really she did, ha?

Male Caller- Yes. (the caller hangs up the phone)

> Raymond is angry he walks into the bathroom,
> pull the curtains.

Paula- (covers her body and angrily says) What the hell is wrong with you? Can't you see I am taking a shower, now get lost.

Raymond-Who the fuck is Calvin?

Paula- I don't know, why are you asking me that?

Raymond- I am going to ask you one more time, who the fuck is Calvin?

Paula- You better pull the shower curtain back, I am freezing and I do not know what you are talking about. I do not know any Calvin.

Raymond- Calvin just called here looking for you.

Paula- I do not know what you are talking about. So get out of my face.

> Raymond (in a rage) grabs her by the hair and
> pulls her out of the shower, naked.

Paula- (screams) Aaaah! Aaah! You are hurting me.
Get your fucking hands off of me.

Raymond- You lying bitch, how dare you? (as he drags her into the bedroom)

Paula- (screaming and yelling, aaaah aaaah) Raymond get your fucking hands off of me. What are you doing? Let go of me and my hair.

Paula is lying on the floor naked, she gets up

Raymond- I am doing what I should have done years ago. I am doing exactly what you want me to do. Don't you ever disrespect me like that again. You are a lying tramp, you have another man calling my motherfucking house and you are lying to me. Bitch get out! This is the last straw.

Paula- (is sacred and crying) What? What? What are you talking about? (she begins to cry) I do not know any Calvin.

Raymond- I want you out of my house right now, you lying bitch. Matter of fact, I am going to leave to let off some steam, cause if I stay around I am going to kill you. Do me a favor; do not be here when I return.

Paula looks shocked and scared. Raymond leaves the house. Paula slowly gets up from off the floor and grabs a robe, she dials Calvin.

Calvin- Hello.

Paula- You dumb motherfucker, how dare you call my house? I gave you my cell number. How did you get my home number?

Calvin- I don't call bitches on their cell. I look folks up. I looked you up and I saw you had a home phone so I called it.

Paula- Don't ever call my house again.

Calvin- You don't have to worry about that wench, because I don't deal with lying Heffas. Have a nice life.

> Calvin hangs up the phone. Paula calls her best friends Sheila.

Sheila- Hey, Girl.

Paula- (crying) Hey, I need your help

Sheila- Paula what is wrong? Why are you crying?

Paula- It's a long story, Girl.

Sheila- You had better tell me.

Paula- You remember that guy I met at the night club last week?

Sheila- Yeah that fine, tall, black beast. What did he do? Did he hurt you?

Paula- He called the house and Raymond answered.

Sheila- Girl, are you stupid? You never give a man your home number.

Paula- I didn't. I gave him my cell but he looked me up and my home number is listed.

Sheila- Damn, Girl. So what happened?

Paula- Raymond answered the phone and they had a discussion.

Sheila- Damn, that is fucked up.

Paula- He wants me out of the house. I need to stay with you for awhile until he calms down.

Sheila- No problem. You can stay as long as you like.

Paula- Thanks, Sheila. I will call you when I am leaving.

Sheila- Okay.

Scene 10

Mark and Monisha are lying in bed relaxing. The phone has been ringing but Monisha refuses to answer.

Mark- Why don't you answer the phone? You know most of the calls are for you.

Monisha- That is exactly the reason why I do not answer, I do not want to be bothered. I just want to lay here all day with my man, no correction soon to be husband. So what are we doing today, Honey?

Mark- (annoyed) I am not laying in bed with you all day. I have things to do today Monisha.

Monisha- (angry) Why not? Why can't we lie in bed all day and relax?

Mark- Like I said, I have things to do, Mo. Aren't you hanging out with your friends today? Don't you have errands to run?

Monisha- Yes I made plans with them for Girls' night out, but I would rather spend time with you. Is that so wrong?

Mark- Yes, we spend at a lot of time together. I do not have time to lie around in bed all day with you. Damn, Girl.

Monisha- Damn what? You know most men would love to lie in bed all day with their woman.

Mark- Really, well I am not one of those men, I have errands to run and I have things to do. (Mark sits up in the bed)

Monisha- Baby, we are engaged we need to spend time together, because when we get married it's going to be just you and me all of the time.

Mark- I think you should hang out with your friends Mo. I think you should go out and take care of your errands. Aren't you working out today with your trainer?

Monisha- (annoyed) Why don't you want to spend time with your soon to be wife? I don't feel like working out. I just want to lie in bed with you. We can just chill and watch movies, and we can make a marathon out of it.

Mark- You are not hearing me so I am going to take a shower, I have a lot to do today.

Monisha- (raising her voice, even more annoyed and pointing her fingers in Mark's face) That is fucked up that my fiancé does not want to spend time with me.

Mark- First of all you need to calm down, and stop raising your voice at me. Second of all don't ever point your finger in my face again, you got that? Thirdly we spend time together all the time, but I have a life Mo and you should have one or get one.

Monisha- So what, you need your space?

Mark- In a way yes. You had a life before me didn't you?

> He walks into the bathroom and takes a shower,
> Monisha follows him saying,

Monisha- Yes I did Mark, but that was before we got engaged.

Mark- All I am saying is do not get rid of your friends because you are engaged, do not stop doing things for yourself, it's crazy.

Monisha- You know I am so sick and tired of you not wanting to spend time with me, all I want to do is please you and spend time with you, is that so wrong? Now you are calling me crazy.

Mark- I don't have time for all this bickering.

Monisha- Oh so it's like that ha, Mark?

Mark- See, there you go taking shit the wrong way and taking it personal.

Monisha- No, no I get it, at first you chased after me, saying you wanted me and needed me, now I am available to you around the clock, you are getting tired of me. I don't get it.

> Mark continues to take his shower and does not respond.

Monisha- Now you are going to ignore me.

Mark- Look it's obvious you want to argue, and I am not interested in doing that.

Monisha- If this is how it's going to be being married to you then I need to really consider if I can handle this.

Mark- I feel the same way. I am not going to be arguing over stilly stuff. I don't have time for drama, Monisha.

> He gets out of the shower, grabs a towel and walks back into the bedroom. He begins to put on some sweats.

Monisha- Oh so it's like that, huh?

Mark- Girl, what are you talking about? He grabs his keys and wallet.

Monisha- Oh so now you are going to walk out on me, I am so glad I am getting to see the real Mark Richardson.

> Mark continues to ignore Monisha, at times he shakes his head in disbelief. He puts on his watch.

Monisha- Where the hell are you going?

Mark- (looks up at Monisha) The last time I checked, my mother was living in Chicago, but to answer your question so this does not escalate even further, I am going to the gym to workout; something I do every weekend with my buddies. Then I am going to run some errands.

Monisha- You know that buddy thing is going to have to stop once we get married.

Mark- Excuse me?

Monisha- You heard me. You need to stop spending so much time with your buddies and more time with me, your fiancée.

Mark- You know what, I am not even going to respond to that, cause you are tripping. You must be on your cycle or something.

> Mark walks to the door and Monisha throws the phone at him, the phone misses his head by an inch.

Mark- (turns around in shock) You know what? These little girl tantrums need to stop, don't be here when I get back, Monisha.

Monisha- What the hell does that mean? Don't be home! Why? So you can bring some bitch up in here?

Mark walks out of the room shaking his head in disbelief; he grabs his gym bag and his cell phone, Monisha screams after him as he leaves

Monisha- Mark! Mark! Don't ignore me, Mark!

Mark slams the bedroom door as he walks downstairs. He walks out the front door and to his black Lincoln Navigator. Monisha runs behind him calling him all kinds of names, screaming and yelling as he walks towards his car, she is yelling in the drive way.

Monisha- You black bastard, fuck you I don't need you, Mark!

Monisha comes inside and calls Kim.

Kim- Hello.

Monisha- (sounding sad) Hey you.

Kim- You do not sound so hot. Are you okay?

Monisha- Yes.

Kim- Are you sure? You know that you can talk to me.

Monisha- I know but it's no biggie.

Kim- Are you coming out with us tonight?

Monisha- No, I don't think so.

Kim- Why? Do you have plans?

Monisha- No, I don't.

Kim- Then what is the problem? We are doing our Girls' night out like we do every month.

Monisha- I am not sure.

Kim- What are you doing now?

Monisha- Nothing.

Kim- Come to Salon Toure. Sharon and I are here getting pampered.

Monisha- No, I am going to pass. Look, I will talk to you later.

Kim- Okay, I hope you change your mind about later.

Monisha- Yeah, okay I will talk to you later.

Kim- Bye.

Sharon- (sitting in salon chair next to Kim, she is soaking her feet and hears the conversation with Kim and Monisha) Let me guess, she is not coming.

Kim- I don't think so.

Sharon- (shaking her head) What else is new? She needs to give the brother some space.

Kim- Yeah, since she got engaged she rarely comes out.

Sharon- Suffocating the brother is what she is doing. I have already talked to her but she does not listen.

Kim- Yeah she really does not.

Sharon- Look, we need to relax and enjoy our pedicure.

Kim- Yep, but let me call Karen.

Sharon- I already did, I told you.

Kim- You know that she is forgetful, let me just reconfirm.

> Kim is on her cell calling her other girlfriend Karen. Karen is single and believes all men are gay, bisexual, married or playas. Karen picks up the phone.

Karen- Hello, Kim.

Kim- Hey Karen, how are you doing Girl?

Karen- I am fine.

Kim-How are the men treating you?

Karen- Please let's not go there.

Kim- Are you coming out tonight?

Karen- (surprised) Tonight! What is happening tonight?

Kim- Girls' night out.

Karen- Shit, I totally forgot, I was so busy trying to get my act together for my date tonight. I will cancel; he was probably gay anyway.

Kim- There you go always being negative, stop claiming those negative things.

Karen- What time are we meeting?

Kim- 7:30 pm.

Karen- I will be there.

Kim- Okay, see you later.

Karen- Bye.

Sharon- So is she coming?

Kim- Yes.

Sharon- Good. Let's get back to our pedicures.

Kim- I agree.

Scene 11

Kim pulls up at the restaurant Tivolies, she pulls up to the valet in her red Porche listening to some Mary J Blige, *Take Me As I Am*. The valet comes to her car. Kim is wearing a short, white silk dress, low V neck and black stilettos, her hair is out.

Valet #1- Good evening Ma'am.

Kim- Hi, good evening.

> He gives her a ticket for her car and takes the keys, he is looking at Kim like he just wants to eat her up, he looks at her finger and sees that she is married.

Valet #1- Your husband is a lucky man Ma'am, enjoy your dinner.

Kim- (blushes) Thank you.

> Kim walks towards the restaurant, she walks in and is greeted by the maitre'd Jean Paul.

Jean Paul- Well, if it isn't the beautiful Mrs. Stevenson.

Kim- Hello Jean Paul, how are you? They both kiss each other on the cheeks twice.

Jean Paul- After seeing you, just peachy.

Kim- You should have reservations for four.

Jean Paul- Yes I do, you are the first to arrive.

Kim- As usual.

Jean Paul- (gestures with his hands) This way please.

Kim follows him to their table.

Jean Paul- (pulls out her chair) Have a wonderful dinner, the waiter will be right with you.

Kim- Thank you, Jean Paul.

Waiter comes right over.

Waiter- Good evening, my name is Vino and I will be your server this evening. What can I get you?

Kim- A glass of water and a bottle of your best wine.

Waiter- Sure.

Waiter comes back with her water and a bottle of Moet, chilled in a bucket.

Kim- Thank you.

Waiter pours the wine in a glass for Kim

Kim- Thanks, Vino.

Waiter- My pleasure, can I be of more assistance?

Kim- Thanks but not right now, I am still waiting for three other guests.

Waiter- Okay, I will check back with you later.

> Kim sips on the wine as she checks her blackberry. Kim has been sitting there for fifteen minutes and no one has arrived, she just chills and takes another sip.
> Sharon pulls up in a red Hummer, playing LL Cool J, *Head Sprung,* as she sings along. Sharon (singing as she pulls up to the valet) going to get your head sprung, your head sprung, the valet smiles as she pulls up with the music blasting.

Valet #1- Nice ride.

Sharon- Thanks.

Valet #1- Must be your husband's?

Sharon- (rolling her eyes) It was his car. This is just part of the alimony honey, just part of it Baby.

Valet- Oh, I am so sorry, I didn't... (before he could finish she interrupts)

Sharon- Please, there is nothing to be sorry about, this is a time of celebration, of partying (she throws the keys at him saying) take care of my baby.

Valet #1- (smiles) You can count on it.

> Sharon is wearing a black lace lingerie looking spaghetti strap V neck dress and black stilettos.

Jean Paul- Lord have mercy.

Sharon - Hello there, Jean Paul.

Jean Paul- Heeeello to you too, you look fantastic.

Sharon- Thank you, Jean Paul.

Jean Paul- (gestures) Follow me this way. Mrs. Stevenson is already here.

Sharon- Of course.

> Jean Paul walks Sharon to her seat and pulls out her chair. Sharon gives Kim a hug.

Kim-You look great.

Sharon- So do you.

Sharon- Sorry I am late, but my man wanted a little appetizer before I left out, you know how that is.

Kim- Hey, you got to cater to him, I ain't mad at you.

Sharon- (looks at the wine bottle) Damn Kim, this shit is almost finished.

Kim- Hello, I've been sitting her for half and hour now waiting for you all, what do you expect?

Sharon- To have some damn wine left over for us.

> They both laugh.

Sharon- (asking Kim) Have you called the others?

Kim- Monisha called me, she is coming.

Sharon- What! She is actually coming up for air?

Kim- You are so wrong. Karen should be here in a few.

Sharon- Well let's get another bottle of wine, since you have already killed this one.

Kim- Sounds like a good idea.

> Monisha pulls up in her gray Escalade, she is
> playing R Kelly, *In The Closet*.

Valet #1- (says to Valet # 2) These women ain't playing tonight. Did you see the one earlier with the red Hummer?

Valet #2- Yes I did.

Valet #1- She is recently divorced and that was her ex's truck, man, she looks hard core.

Valet #2- Yeah looks like she would fuck a nigger's shit up if he fucked around on her.

Valet #1- Yeah, I got that vibe from her, too.

Valet #2- Looks like here is another one of the crew. They must be having a male bashing night out.

> Both men laugh.
> Monisha pulls up to the valet and gets out wear-
> ing a very tight fitting yellow tube top dress and
> open toe stilettos.

Valet #3- (says to Valet #2) My dick just got hard.

Valet #4- Yeah, mine too.

Valet #1- Man, their outfits are out of this world.

Valet #3- And so are they.

> They all laugh.
> As Monsiha approaches, Valet # 1 greets her.

Valet #1- Good evening, Ma'am.

Monisha- Please call me Monisha or Mo. (she hands him over her keys)

Monisha- If my truck is scratched when I return, you and I will have conversations, understood?

Valet #1- Understood, enjoy your evening.

Monisha- I plan on it.

Valet #2- What was her problem?

Valet #1- I don't know, but whatever she wants I will give it to her.

> They both laugh.

Jean Paul- Good evening, how are you doing this wonderful evening?

Monisha- I am doing great, Jean Paul, it's good seeing you.

Jean Paul- I will take you to your table.

> Monisha follows Jean Paul to the table where Kim and Sharon are laughing and having a good time, he pulls out her chair.

Monisha- Thank you.

> Before she sits down she hugs both Kim and Sharon.

Sharon- My, my! We did not think you would come out tonight. And what type of function did you think you were coming to? You are just having dinner with your girlfriends not going out on a first date.

Monisha- Whatever, hater.

Sharon- Hater! Child please.

Kim- Okay, let's not start.

Karen pulls up in her white 355 BMW with the sun roof down, she is listening to Kym's song, *When Love Calls*; she pulls up to the valet.

Valet #1- (saying to Valet #2) She looks like the quiet one.

As Karen pulls up Valet #1 greets her.

Valet #1- Good evening.

Karen- Hello, how are you?

Valet #1- I am great and you?

Karen- (smiling) Wonderful, thanks for asking. (she then hands him her keys)

Karen is wearing a silk print spaghetti strap top with her back out, and two strings tied to the back of the top, and a silk flared skirt to match.

Valet #2- Did you see the ass on her?

Valet #1- It was not hard to miss.

Karen walks to toward the restaurant.

Jean Paul- Good evening, Karen.

Karen- Good evening Jean Paul, how are you?

Jean Paul- Lord I am just speechless, you women are all so beautiful.

Karen- Thanks, I take it everyone is here.

Jean Paul- Yes. (he escorts her to the table, he pulls out her chair)

Karen- Thanks, Jean Paul.

> Before she sits down, she greets everyone by giving them a hug.

Karen- We look good, ya'll.

Sharon- I will drink to that.

Kim- Wait, wait, before we go drinking, lets make a toast. Here is to friendship, everyone needs good friends.

> Everyone raises their glass and toasts.

Karen- Here is to no more gay or bisexual men.

> Everyone just looks at her.

Sharon- You are the only one here that is single and looking, everyone else got a man.

Monisha- What kind of a toast is that?

Karen- Whatever, like I was saying here is to no more gay men for me.

> Everyone laughs.

Sharon- Let's order, I am starved.

Kim- Sounds like a good idea to me.

Waiter- (comes to the table) Are you all ready to order?

Kim- Yes. For appetizers we are going to get Buffalo wings and the spinach and artichoke dip for starters.

Waiter- Okay, coming right up.

Sharon- Can we get three glasses of water please.

Waiter- Sure.

Kim- Okay, so what is the latest from everyone?

Sharon- Let's go around the table, everyone tell us what is the latest since our last gathering.

Sharon- Shit I will start. You all know that I just ended a painful and bitter divorce with that motherfucker.

Kim- Woo! Woo! Sharon take it easy.

Sharon- Is just that every time I think of him cheating on me I just want to scream. Aaaaaaaaaaaaaaaaaaaaaaaaaah that mother-fucker.

Monisha- You did have a choice, you could have forgiven him.

Sharon- Excuse me! Is she stupid?

Monisha- You could have forgiven him, no one is perfect and men will cheat from time to time, but if you really love him you should forgive him and try to work things out.

Sharon- Would you forgive Mark if he cheated on you?

Monisha- First of all Mark will never cheat on me. I satisfy all his desires. I cater to my man twenty four seven.

Sharon- More like stifle your man.

Monisha- Whatever hater, at least I got a man and know how to keep him.

Kim- Okay let's move on, let's change the subject.

Sharon- No let's stay on this subject, this trick thinks because she barely got engaged at 35 after years of searching she is the shit. Well let me refresh your memory.

Sharon- First of all, not too long ago you used to call me, actually all of us crying wondering why men were fucking leaving you, or why he would not commit to you. So now you finally lucked out on a man, you think you are the shit. Well let me tell you something Honey, it's not going to last, just like all your other relationships because you do not understand a man. You complain all the time and you do not give a brother space. Men need their space, Honey.

Monisha- Well apparently you gave Derrick too much space, cause the nigger left you for someone else. Hmm and I think she was much younger, too.

> Sharon jumps out of her seat towards Monisha,
> Kim jumps up to hold her back.

Sharon- What did this bitch just say? I know she ain't talking shit to me.

Kim- Okay, let's change the subject, let's talk about something else.

Karen- Yes, let's talk about why most men are bisexual and gay.

Kim- Okay Karen, we are not going to talk about that, either.

Sharon- No, let me set this bitch straight.

Karen- Please, stop with the profanity.

Sharon- First of all, I was engaged three times before the age of 30, Honey, two I turned down the last one I accepted and we lasted for 13 years, and I refuse to forgive a man that will risk losing 13 years of memories and a beautiful family for some ass. Sorry I can't do it. But you won't know anything about that. You never will.

Karen- What about you, Kim?

Kim- What about me?

Karen- If Michael...

Kim- (interrupts before she could finish) If Michael what? First of all let's not talk it up all right; I don't think Michael will ever cheat on me.

Sharon- Girl never say never, men are Dogs.

Kim- Not all men cheat. I just don't think Michael will do that to me.

Sharon- The question is would you forgive him or divorce him?

Kim- (sips on her wine) See that is a tough question, it depends on the situation.

Karen- (shocked) Depends on the situation? Girl, what are you talking about?

Kim- Like I said, it depends on the situation.

Sharon- Cheating is cheating it does not matter what the circumstances are.

Kim- (changes the conversation by asking Monisha) So tell us about the wedding, have you set a date? What are the colors? Give us details.

Monisha- (gets excited) The colors will be pastel, not sure about the style. The dates is set for June 11th, I have got to be a June bride.

Karen- What about your bridal party? How many bridesmaids will you have?

Monisha- Seven.

Sharon- Seven! That's a big wedding party so are we in it? Do tell.

> Monisha takes a long sip of her wine and says nothing.

Sharon- So are we in the wedding or what?

Monisha- Actually, no.

Sharon- What? You were all were in my wedding, why can't we be in yours?

Monisha- I just don't want any married or divorced folks in my wedding.

Sharon- (shouts out loud) Excuse me! Bitch, you got a lot of nerve; do you all hear this bullshit?

Kim- I can understand, most people are that way. But I know Karen is a bridesmaid, after all, she introduced you to Mark.

> Monisha takes a much longer sip of her wine, and
> puts her head down.

Karen- What, I am not in the wedding?

Sharon- I told you that this bitch was trippin.

Monisha- If you call me a bitch one more time, I swear.

Sharon- You swear what?

Kim- Okay, okay let's all chill.

Monisha-Yes, Karen introduced me to Mark, but Karen you are very negative. You are always talking about people, calling folks gay or bisexual and you are loud about it and you don't care. I do not want any negativity on my wedding day. I'm sorry.

Sharon- No she didn't go there.

Karen- (angry) You ungrateful, selfish bitch.

Sharon- Yeah, give it to her.

Kim- Sharon, stop.

Sharon- Stop what, she is wrong Kim. Karen introduced Monisha to her best friend Mark, and the least she could do was put her ass in the wedding. That is foul.

Karen- Correction, my ex.

Monisha-(shocked) What!

Sharon- Oh this shit is getting good. (she gestures to the waiter) Another bottle of Moet, please.

Waiter- Coming right up.

Sharon- I have to drink to this one, Lord have mercy.

Kim- Sharon, stop stirring the pot.

Monisha- What did you say Karen?

Kim- Hold up Karen. I thought Mark was your best friend.

Karen- That's right, Mark is my ex and I told you he was my best friend because I know you would not date an ex of mine.

Monisha- You damn right I would not.

Sharon- (laughing) This shit is too funny.

Kim- Sharon, come on.

Monisha- Your ass is lying. Mark would never date a person like you. You are not his type, Honey.

Karen- Excuse you. A person like me? Oh you think you are the shit now ha, Mo? Well we dated, we did it all. I know he likes his woman freaky, he loves eating the kitty cat, and he loved eating mine. Oh I know everything about him. So before you get cocky and suggest he would not date someone like me, you need to ask him.

Sharon- Lord have mercy. I say we need another bottle of wine up in here. It's going to be a long night.

Monisha- I don't have to ask my man, I know his taste and you are not it.

Karen- Funny, I said the same thing when he told me he thought you were cute. So yes, you have my leftovers.

Sharon- (laughs) That is what she gets. Let her have it, Karen.

Monisha- Fuck you, Sharon.

Sharon- I bet you would love to wouldn't you? I always knew you were a closet Lesbian, but sorry I am strictly dickly.

Kim- Okay, okay, this is getting way out of hand, and all this cursing needs to stop. Come on people we are friends here.

Karen- With friends like her, who needs enemies?

Sharon- I will drink to that.

Kim- Karen, why did you set up your ex with Monisha? And why didn't you tell her he was your ex?

Karen- I know everything about Mark. We dated four years ago; things did not work out but we remained great friends, he is like a brother to me. Mark thought Monisha was cute and asked me to hook them up. Apparently, I made a very big mistake.

Sharon- (sipping on her wine) A very big one, Lord have mercy. (she takes another sip)

Kim- Shut up Sharon. I would never set up my best friend with my ex. It's just nasty.

Karen- Like I said, we dated a long time ago, it was not recent. Mark is like a brother to me. He told me he wanted to meet her. What was I supposed to do?

Sharon- Not introduce him to her.

Kim- Sharon, please.

Monisha- You wish you knew everything about him.

Karen- Whatever. I am not going to sit here and argue with you about it. The two of you have only been together for two years.

Monisha- Exactly, and I got the ring and you did not.

Karen- And your point is?

Monisha- I don't want you in my wedding.

Sharon- Your ass needs to be glad she hooked you up, if not you would still be single to this day. Crying to us and shit about how men are dogging you out. So in actuality you owe Karen, at least a thank you.

Monisha- I do not owe her anything.

Sharon- Monisha, you are such a bitch and obviously do not know the meaning of friendship.

Monisha- You have one more time to call me a bitch Sharon and I swear I am going to kick your ass.

Sharon- I wish you would.

Kim- Stop, let's stop it. We are acting like high school folks here and this is silly. Now if Monisha does not want us in her wedding, as her friends we should respect that. Let's act mature here.

Monisha- (excuses herself) I will be right back.

Kim- Okay.

Sharon- She is such a bitch. She looks awfully skinny; she is probably starving to get into the dress.

Kim- Come on let's not talk about the girl behind her back.

Karen- She is probably going to call Mark to find out if this is true.

Kim- You think so?

Karen- I know so.

Sharon- (laughs) How pathetic.

Kim- You all need to stop.

Sharon- Stop what, Kim?

Karen- I am no longer her friend, that's a wrap.

Monisha returns from the bathroom.

Kim- I was just coming to check up on you, are you okay?

Monisha- Look, I hate to be rude, but I have to leave.

Kim- Sorry to hear that Mo, is everything okay?

Monisha- Everything is fine; I just don't feel well all of a sudden.   (reaches over and hugs Kim) My apologies, it was good seeing you Kim.

Monisha literally runs out the restaurant without hugging Karen or Sharon.

Karen- I guess we don't get hugs.

Sharon- I guess not, but who cares.

Kim- Damn, that is really unfortunate.

Sharon- What is unfortunate?

Kim- That Monisha got all upset and left.

Karen- Oh well, that's on her.

Kim- I cannot believe you two.

Sharon- What! What did we do? We are still here.

Kim- You guys instigated shit with her.

Karen- Whatever!

Sharon- So what's going on with you Karen?

Karen- Well, I have been dating the same guy now for three months, and I am proud to say that he is not on the DL or maried as of yet.

Sharon- So how is the sex?

Karen- I don't know?

Sharon- What do you mean you don't know?

Karen- We haven't had sex yet, it's only been three months, and he needs to work for the vagina.

Kim- (laughs) I know that is right.

Sharon- Bullshit, you need to find out what you are working with. You do not have time to waste.

Karen- Whatever, Sharon you are so crazy.

Kim- Well what's going on with you Sharon?

Sharon- Well I have a new man, that's right, we have been together now for three weeks and yes the sex is good, and he is better than my ex.

Karen- Alrighty then.

Kim- Three weeks and you had sex already?

Sharon- Yes, you got a problem with that?

Karen- Yeah, that is way too fast. You are such a slut.

Sharon- Look we are grown there is no need to play games, plus I need to know what I am working with.

Kim- So who is this guy? How and where did you meet him?

Sharon- You all are going to love this, he is Tyler's basketball coach.

Karen- Oh Lord, your son's coach.

Sharon- Yep.

Kim- Sharon, that is ridiculous.

Sharon- What is so ridiculous about that?

Kim- Does Tyler know?

Sharon- Of course not, Tyler does not need to know anything, he is only 13.

Kim- That is trifling.

Karen- Does Derrick know?

Sharon- Who gives a fuck about him? He is an ex honey. I don't care what he thinks.

Karen- You are so over the top. How did you all hook up?

Sharon- At one of Tyler's games. We have been attracted to and flirting with each other for quite some time but we were both involved. Now that we are both divorced, it's on and popping.

Kim- Lord have mercy.

Karen- What has been going on with you, Kim?

Kim- Not sure if I can top all the new men and good sex stuff. Michael and I are celebrating our ten year anniversary next week and we are throwing a party, your invitations are in the mail.

Karen- That's awesome.

> Waiter brings the main course and they are all eating and talking.

Kim- Thank you.

Waiter- Just call me Vino.

Sharon- Okay.

Vino- What happened to the other girl?

Kim- She had to go, but we will pay for her food.

Vino- No, that's okay I will take it off the bill.

Karen- Thanks, Vino

Vino- Enjoy your meal.

SCENE 12

Mark and his boys are hanging out getting ready for the fight to come on, Mark's cell rings again; it has been ringing all day. Mark looks at his phone, it's Monisha. He ignores the call.

Marcus- Damn someone is blowing up your phone.

Terrell- Yeah Man, you need to answer it or turn it off.

Keith- Shit do something, it's really annoying.

Terrell- So who is blowing up your cell like that Man, your moms?

      Everyone laughs.

Terrell- It's Monisha Man, I can bet some money on it.

Mark- Yes, you are right.

Keith- Man, she is on you hard.

Terrell- I told you what to do, Man. See you should have nipped that in the bud from the get go. Stacey knows that when I am out with my boys I am out with my boys; do not call me unless it's an emergency.

Keith- You see I don't have that problem; Carla always had a life outside of me. I used to be the one blowing up her phone when we were dating, she gave me my space, shit sometimes too much space, but I appreciate her and have much love for her because she allows me to be me. She does not trip asking me questions like where you are going? Who you been with and all that shit.

Charles- See I agree with Terrell, don't be blowing up my phone unless the house is on fire. Women need to get a life and stop trying to be with their men twenty four seven.

Mark- Well she can't seem to understand that. She wants to be with me twenty four seven. She has to know my every move.

Terrell- Don't marry her, Man. If she is acting up like this now, things are going to get worse.

Keith- He is right, Man.

Charles- What you see is what you get.

Keith- What do you like about her?

Mark pauses.

Keith- Damn Man, why do you have to pause? I just asked a simple question.

Mark- I can tell you what I used to like, lately Man we do so much arguing, I do not know what I like about her anymore.

Charles- Sounds like major trouble, don't marry this chick, Man. You all got some serious issues you need to work out.

Tony- I say use my tactic.

Terrell, Charles and Keith- (all ask) What the hell is that?

Tony- Slap the bitch.

Mark- What?

Terrell- Man, you are crazy.

Tony- Did I stutter? I said to slap the bitch, you see Melanie and I have been together for a year, one time she got loud with me and threw water in my face calling me a punk. I slapped her so hard that was the last time she stepped out of line.

Keith- What? That is crazy.

Terrell- If you have to slap her you do not need to be with her, we don't get down like that, we do not hit our ladies.

Tony- It works for me.

Keith- Yeah you are the only one that does that shit and it ain't cute, Man.

Tony- It works. Did my phone ring once? Nope. Melanie knows that I am out with the fellas and I get home when I get home. Don't be calling me even if the house is on fire. I respect her and have never given her any reason not to trust me. I do not disrespect her; I just ask in return she does the same.

Mark- Well I have never hit Monisha and I do not plan on doing that.

Keith- You two need to get some counseling. That is what Tiffany and I did before we got married. We laid it out and it has helped.

Mark- Look, I do not want to talk about my fiancée anymore, we are here to watch the fight so let's do that, where is the Budweiser?

Terrell- That is what I am talking about.

> Keith gets up and goes to the refrigerator to grab some Budweiser. Mark's cell rings again.

Tony- Damn Man, this shit is annoying. What is her deal?

Keith- Man, answer your phone or put that shit on vibrate. The fight is on.

Terrell- You need to answer it because it looks like she is going to call you until you do.

Marcus- I say turn the damn thing off.

> They all laugh.
> Monisha leaves a nasty message. Monisha hits redial and calls back, Mark does not answer the phone. Monisha leaves another angry message.

Tony- Looks like you've got quite a few messages. Play the shit so your boys can analyze it for you.

Mark- (plays the message on speaker) I am just going to play one.

> Mark dials his voicemail, you have ten new messages.

Keith- Ten! Ten messages Man. That shit is crazy.

> Message ten from Monisha plays,

Monisha- You black motherfucker I have left you ten messages and your black ass can't return my calls. Fuck you Mark. You are probably fucking some bitch. What kind of a man does not return any of his fiancée's phone calls? Fuck you, don't come home tonight.

Terrell- Ouch!

Keith- Wow! That is crazy, Man. I could not deal with that.

Charles- Damn, what is her problem? Sounds like she needs some, Brother you need to handle yours.

Tony- Just beat her.

Keith- Tony, shut the fuck up. Hitting a woman is not the answer. Stop talking that crazy shit in my house, Man. (to Mark) Look, it's your house, Man. Damn, she is telling you not to come home to your house? That is fucked up.

Mark- See, that is the kind of thing that turns me off about her.

Charles- Why is she calling you so often?

Mark- We had an argument this morning and she threw a phone at me. The shit missed my head by an inch.

Keith- (shocked) What!

Mark- I know, Man.

Keith- I won't return her call, and I won't return home tonight. I will teach her ass a lesson, and when I do return I will ask her to leave.

Mark- Look, I am turning off my phone so I can watch the fight. (he turns off his phone)

Scene 13

It's Monday morning and Monisha rolls over in the bed and realizes that Mark is not in bed, she walks into the guest room, the living room and the other spare room and she realizes he did not come home. He has been gone since Sunday night. She then goes upstairs to check her cell phone for messages, there are no messages. She checks the home phone and there are no messages there either.

Monisha- (angry) That motherfucker. Where the fuck is he?

Monisha calls Mark's cell phone, but the call goes to voicemail. She tries to leave a message but his voicemail box is full.

Monisha- Oh your mail box is full ha, then I am going to text your ass, nobody ignores me. I can't believe this bastard spent the night out.

Mark is sitting in his car, he sits contemplating on what he is going to do and how he is going to handle Monisha. He turns on his phone. R

Kelly's, *If I Can Turn Back The Hand Of Time*, is
playing in the background. His phones rings and
it's his secretary Missy.

Mark- Hello.

Missy- Hello Mr. Williams, I hate to call you on your cell, but
your 9:00 a.m. conference call has be rescheduled for 11:00 a.m.
and Mr. Hughman wanted me to double check to see if that is
okay with you.

Mark- I will be out of the office today so please cancel all of my
appointments for today. And reschedule the conference call for
tomorrow.

Missy- Okay.

Mark- Thanks Missy, see you in the morning.

Mark hangs up the phone and heads home, he
pulls up at his house and put the keys in the door
and the door would not open.

Mark- What the hell?

He put the keys in the door again but nothing.

Mark- What the fuck is going on here? No this bitch did not
change the locks on my door. No she didn't. Okay it's on.

Mark jumps back into his car, pulls up at Ellerby
locksmith.

Mark- I cannot believe this shit.

Mark walks into the locksmith's.

Manager- Good morning, how can I help you?

Mark- I need to change a lock on a door.

Manager- What kind of door? Car, office or house.

Mark- I need to change the locks on my house.

Manager- Okay, I will need the address, so fill out this form.

Mark- I need to have this done today, like now.

Manager- That is not a problem, Sir.

> Mark completes the form and gives it to the manager.

Manager- Okay we can leave right now and take care of this.

Mark- Great, you can follow me.

> Monisha is heading home she looks at her cell phone and there are no missed calls or any calls from Mark. She pulls up in the driveway and she does not see Mark's car, she pulls into the garage and his car is not there either. She enters the front door and realizes the door is already open. She is a bit startled; she assumes she must have forgotten to lock the door.

Monisha- I do recall locking the front door, maybe I did not.

> Monisha walks over to the phone and there are two messages, she is excited.

Monisha- It's about time he called; I wonder what he has to say.

> She plays the messages but none are from Mark. She heads upstairs and is startled to see Mark sitting on the bed.

Monisha- (jumps in astonishment and drops her keys) Oh my God Mark, you scared the shit of me.

Mark just sits there.

Monisha- What are you doing here?

Mark- Remember, I live here.

Monisha- I mean how did you get in?

Mark- Yeah, I know that you changed the looks on the door, how dare you? Who the fuck do you think you are?

Monisha is scared she has never seen Mark this angry.

Monisha- Why are you cursing at me, Honey, please calm down. What was I supposed to do? You disappear for two days and you did not return any of my calls.

Mark- This is my house, you just stay here and as of now you are no longer welcome here.

Monisha- (shocked) What are you talking about? This is our house.

Mark- Get out!

Monihsa- This is crazy Mark, we need to talk.

Mark- We have nothing to talk about. You see those boxes over there? Your things are in there. I want you out.

Monisha- (looks to the floor and there are five boxes with her things in it) Mark what are you doing?

Mark- It's over, Monisha.

Monisha- (screaming and crying all at the same time) This is fucked up Mark, you cannot do this to me.

Mark- I just did, now get out of my house.

Monisha- But I have nowhere to go.

Mark- That is not my problem.

Monisha- Mark please. Please, Honey. I love you. Please let's talk about it.

Mark- There is nothing to say.

> Monisha rushes towards him in anger, she tries to slap him, he grabs her hands and pins her against the wall.

Mark- Don't even try it. I have never laid a hand on you, but I swear if you touch me or hit me, you are going to regret it. Now you can leave on your own, or I can literally throw you out. Which do you prefer?

Monisha- You fucking bastard, you are going to pay for this, oh this is not over.

Mark- Save the threats, Mo. It's over. Oh and by the way you can keep the ring as a souvenir.

Monisha- You are such an asshole. (she continues crying) I have nowhere to go.

Mark- Sounds like a personal problem to me. I hear something; that must be the moving truck. It's just in time because I have somewhere to go within the hour.

Monisha- You rented a moving truck Mark?

Mark- Yes and they are here.

Monisha- Oh you have some other bitch, ha.

Mark- I may, who knows.

Monisha rolls her eyes and gets on her cell phone, she calls Kim.

Kim- Hello.

Monisha- (crying) Oh, Kim.

Kim- Mo, are you okay?

Monisha- No. Mark just threw me out and I have nowhere to go.

Kim- Oh my God. Okay, I will come and get you.

Monisha- You do not need to come and get me, he rented a moving truck and packed up all of my things. Can you believe this shit?

Kim- Oh my God. That is awful.

Monisha- Can I stay at your house?

Kim- Ok course, Mo. Of course, you can stay as long as you need.

Monisha- See you soon.

Mark- Hurry up the truck is waiting and I am paying by the hour.

Monisha- I cannot believe you Mark. This is fucked up and I swear this is not over.

Mark- Okay, whatever.

Mark walks outside and greets the driver.

Mark- Thanks for coming so quickly. We have several boxes inside, just come in and get it.

Mover #1- (asks Monisha) Ma'am do you have an address for where we need to drop off these boxes?

Monisha- (Crying) Yes.

Mover #2- Okay we are all set, let's go.

Mark- (saying to the movers) Thanks, Man. Monisha, you take care now.

Monisha- Fuck you Mark. You have not seen the last of me.

Mark- Gee, I hope so.

Monisha- (calls Kim) I will get to you in 45 minutes.

Kim- I will see you shortly. In the mean time I will get your room set up.

Scene 14

Kim and Michael are lying in bed, Michael rolls over to her and whispers.

Michael- Good morning, Mrs. Stevenson.   Happy ten year anniversary.

Kim- (smiles) Good morning.

Michael- We have been married now for ten years and I still feel like we are on our honeymoon.

Kim- Yes, I feel the same way.

Michael- I love you.

Kim- I love you more. You know what Michael?

Michael- What?

Kim- I was thinking we could celebrate Sasha's birthday and our anniversary next month in Paris.

Michael- Sounds like a great idea. How is Monisha doing?

Kim- She is devastated. She is going to be here for a few weeks, I hope you don't mind.

Michael- No, of course not. I have a surprise for you.

> Michael reaches underneath his pillow and pulls
> out a box and gives it to Kim.

Kim- (excited) Oh, what is it?

Michael- You need to open it up.

Kim- (kisses him, and then opens the box, inside is a beautiful diamond necklace with a heart shaped stone) Ooooh my God Michael, this is gorgeous, thank you Honey, oh thank you.

Michael- No thank you for being the great wife that you are, I really do love you Kim.

Kim- (teary eyed) Oh Michael I love you more.

> Michael puts the necklace around her neck, Kim
> jumps out of bed to go and look in the mirror.

Kim- (touching and admiring the necklace around her neck) This is absolutely gorgeous. I will wear it tonight at the party. We have a busy day planned.

Michael- What time are the caterers coming?

Kim- They will be here around 6 p.m.

Michael- What about the decorators?

Kim- Around 3 pm.

Michael- Looks like we have everything covered.

Kim- Let me go and check on Monisha.

Michael- I will check on the kids.

> Kim walks downstairs to the guest room, she
> knocks on the door.

Kim- Monisha, are you up?

Monisha- Come on in Kim.

Kim- How are you doing, Mo? How did you sleep?

Monisha- I have been up since 5 am. I just could not sleep. Oh what a beautiful necklace.

Kim- Thanks, it's my anniversary gift.

Monisha- It's beautiful. Happy Anniversary.

Monisha begins to cry.

Kim- Don't cry Mo it's going to be okay.

Monisha- I'm sorry it's your anniversary I do not need to spoil it.

Kim- You are not spoiling it. I know you miss Mark. But just give him some time.

Monisha- You are right. What can I help you with?

Kim- Nothing, the caterers and the decorators have everything under control. All we have to do is show up.

Kim- Can I get you some breakfast?

Monisha- No, I am not hungry. Are you ready for tonight?

Kim- Yes, I am so excited. I can't wait to celebrate with family and friends.

Monisha- Me too.

Scene 15

Everyone is arriving, there is a live band, the room is set up with tables of six, all the tables have fresh flowers decorated elegantly, a bottle of Moet, and mint like chocolates are on each table. The waiters are serving hor'dourves. Kim is very excited, she is wearing a long red satin dress with the splits on the side, and her hair is up. The kids are upstairs; this is a party for grown ups and everyone is laughing and having a good time. Kim's parents arrive; Michael goes to greet them.

Michael- Hello Mr. & Mrs. Tucker.

> The father ignores him, however Stephanie speaks.

Stephanie- Hello, Michael.

Mr. Tucker- Where is my daughter?

Michael- Well hello to you to Mr. Tucker, I believe Kim is greeting her guests.

Teddy- Please call me Teddy. Where is our table?

Michael- Oh, you can sit anywhere you choose.

Teddy- Good. (he walks away)

> Everyone has pretty much arrived, except for Kim's brother Kevin. Kim tries to stall before making a toast but she cannot stall anymore. Michael walks up to Kim

Michael- Honey, we need to make a toast, have you heard from Kevin?

Kim- (worried) No, that's not like him. He called 40 minutes ago and he said he was en route.

Michael- Did you try calling him?

Kim- Yes, it went to voicemail. Go ahead Honey, let's make the toast. I just hope he shows up soon.

Michael- (begins to hit his glass) Everyone, we are going to make a toast, please raise your glasses.

> Everyone gathers around with their glass, the caterers are pouring champagne in everyone's glass. Kim and Michael are on stage with the band getting ready to make a toast. During that time Kevin walks through the front door with his partner Tracey. Stephanie smiles, the father Teddy is disgusted he walks out of the room and it's obvious, Kevin sees his dad leaving and calls out to him.

Kevin- Dad! Dad! Where are you going?

> Teddy keeps on walking.

Kevin- Are you embarrassed of me, Dad? Is that what it is?

Kim- (tries to intervene) I am so glad my brother Kevin is here, cheers to Kevin everyone.

> Everyone raises their glasses and says cheers.

Kevin- (hurt) You don't have to be embarrassed Dad, I will leave instead.

Teddy- (stops and turns around) That would be a good idea.

Stephanie- Teddy, stop it. Kevin please do not leave.

> Everyone is looking around, some are talking amongst themselves. Kim is embarrassed.

Kevin- I am sorry for disappointing you. All I have ever wanted was to be loved by you and accepted by you, but you never loved and accepted me.

Stephanie- (tries to interrupt) Oh Son, that is not true.

Kevin- Yes it is Mom, it always has been.

Teddy- I do not need a faggot for a son, you are not my son, I do not have a gay son. How dare you come to your sister's anniversary party with another man. It's sick. You sicken me.

Stephanie- (yelling) Teddy stop it, you stop it right now.

> Everyone in the room is shocked they do not know what to do.

Kim- (begins to cry she turns to Michael) Please Honey, do something.

> Michael walks over to Teddy.

Michael- You are in my house and this is my anniversary party. You will not cause a scene.

Teddy- Then I will leave.

Michael- Suit yourself.

Kim- (yells) No one is leaving; this is my anniversary party. All I wanted was for my friends and family to have a good time and share this special day with us. Dad, this is your son, how can you say this to him?

Teddy- He is not my son. I am sorry if I ruined your party but I am leaving.

Kim- No one is leaving, no one.

Teddy- Look Sweetie, I do not want to cause any more pain or anger so I will just leave.

Kim- Like I said no one is leaving, we are going to toast and have a good time.

> Teddy walks out of the room and heads out of the front door.

Kim- (screams after him) Daddy! Daddy! (her voice breaking)

Michael- (hugs her and says) Its okay, Honey. Let's go back on stage and make a toast to our guests.

> They both walk back on stage.

Michael- Everyone, I apologize but I want to make a toast to my lovely wife whom I love very much. It has been ten wonderful years of marriage, and four years of dating. I knew I was going to marry Kim on our first date. Kim I love you more than life itself. Happy anniversary. Cheers to my wife.

> Everyone says cheers and raises their glass in cheer. Kim is crying.

Michael- (hugging her and whispers in her ears) Come on Honey, pull it together for your guests.

Kim- I am so furious right now. I cannot believe my dad.

Michael- I understand but you need to put on your game face.

Kim- I am so embarrassed.

Michael- So am I but we need to make the best of this.

Kim- (turns to the crowd) I just want to say that I love you Michael, with all of my heart. I don't know what I would do if you were not in my life. I want to thank everyone for coming out, please continue to party.

> Kevin is deeply hurt, his partner Tracey tries to console him.

Tracey- It's going to be okay, Kevin.

Kevin- No its not. For 40 years my own father has hated me. He never wanted me, I was an outcast from birth.

Tracey- Oh Honey, stop it; now is not the time.

Kevin- No its true, Tracey. Oh well you heard it for yourself, he said he does not have a son. (his voice breaks)

Tracey- Just give him some time.

Kevin- Time. He has had forty years, how much more time does he need?

> Stephanie continues to try to reach Teddy but keeps getting his voicemail, she is furious. She cannot believe what he said.
> Kevin walks into the kitchen, Stephanie goes over and hugs him.

Stephanie- Son, I am so sorry. Your dad never meant what he said. He must have been drunk.

Kevin- He meant it, Mom. Its okay, you do not have to cover up for dad or make excuses.

Stephanie- I love you, Honey.

Kevin- I know that, but your love is not enough for two. I need and have always needed the love of my father. I know that you try to give it Mom, I know that you did.

Stephanie- Oh Kevin, I am so sorry.

Kevin- Why Ma? Why dad never want me as a child?

Stephanie- Oh Kevin, this is nonsense.

Kevin- Ma stop it, stop lying to me. This has been eating at me all my life, and I have been struggling with it. Please just tell me, you owe me that.

Stephanie- (looks at him) Oh Kevin, Sweetie.

Kevin- Ma, my own father does not like me. You do not need to protect me, I am a grown man now. I can handle it. Please Ma.

Stephanie- You know what Son, this is not even important. It does not matter. It's silly and irrelevant.

Kevin- It's important to me.

Stephanie- Son let's not go there, it is really not necessary.

Kevin- It's necessary for me, Ma.

Stephanie- Son, your father has a color complex. When he was little his parents treated him like a step child because he was the darker of his five siblings. Your dad never liked you because your skin was darker than the rest of his kids.

Kevin- Thanks Mom, but that is no excuse.

Stephanie- I agree but I wanted you to know where it was stemming from. Look, let's go back out there and celebrate with your sister.

Michael- You see, everyone is having a good time.

Kim- Yes, I am so glad. I wish my dad was here.

Michael- It's going to be okay, do you want to dance?

Kim- Sure.

> They both get on the dance floor and are dancing and having a good time.
> Its three hours later and the party is wrapping up.
> Sharon walks up to Kim and says,

Sharon- This was such a great celebration for your anniversary. Thanks for inviting me. I had a fantastic time.

Kim- (hugs her) Thanks for coming. I love you, Girl.

> Kim hugs Sharon's new man and says,

Kim- Todd, it was nice meeting you finally.

Todd- The pleasure was all mine. I had a great time.

Sharon- Take care.

Kim- Drive carefully.

> They all walk to the front door, Kim still standing at the door, and Karen walks up to Kim and says,

Karen- Kim this was a lovely anniversary party.

Kim- Thanks for coming.

Karen- Don't mention it. Would not have missed this for the world. (they hug each other)

Kim- Thanks Girl, please drive carefully.

Karen- - Girl, my man is picking me up. Actually he is here right now.

Kim- Why didn't you bring him to the party?

Karen- It's a new relationship. I have to make sure he is all right first before I start bringing him around my friends.

Kim- Okay.

> Most of the party guests are leaving and Michael joins Kim at the door to thank the guests for coming.
> All the guest have left and Kim and Michael hug each other.

Michael- Kim Stevenson, I love you more than life itself. Here is to another 10 years.

Kim- I will kiss to that.

> They both embrace each other with a passionate kiss.

Scene 16

FIVE YEARS LATER

Michael has been working late and does not seem like himself. He seems out of it at work, and during meetings. He rarely sleeps at night. He has been going to counseling and thinks he is going through a midlife crisis. His friends are concerned about him. Michael leaves work around 8:00 pm he gets home around 9:00 pm. He has been missing dinner with the family for quite some time now since he has been going to counseling. Kim is not aware of his issues. Kim has not been saying anything about him missing dinner, but on this particular night she decides to. Michael walks in the front door, Kim is sitting at the table drinking a glass of wine, it is apparent she has been drinking for a while now.

Michael- (startled) Well hello Honey, what are you doing up so late?

Kim- What are you doing home so late? (sarcastic) I am sorry, you must have been working as usual.

Michael- That is correct.

Kim- I don't believe you. I am so tired of you coming home at 9 pm, and 10 pm every night. I am sick of it.

Michael- Honey, I have been working.

Kim- Bullshit. What is really going on? I have been calling you and it goes to voicemail. That is not like you Michael. What is going on with you?

Michael- Look, I am tired and I had a long day.

Kim- We need to talk.

Michael- Yes we do but not right now.

Kim- Why not?

Michael- Because it's late and I am tired. I have been going through a lot Kim, you just don't know.

Kim- You are right. I don't know because you do not talk to me about anything anymore. You come home late every damn night and we barely see each other. It's like I have a stranger in my house.

Michael- First of all you have been drinking, so I am not going to talk to you in that state of mind.

Kim- No, we are going to talk now.

Michael- Fine, have it your way. What do you want to talk about?

Kim- Something is obviously wrong here and I want you to tell me what it is.

Michael- I do not know what you are talking about.

Kim- Let me refresh your memory. You don't come home for dinner anymore, you get home at 9 pm or 10 pm every night. You take a shower and go to bed. No sex, no cuddling, no nothing. Do I need to continue?

Michael- No.

Kim- Okay, then what the hell is going on? Now you see why I am drinking.

Michael- I have a lot going on right now, I feel like I am having a nervous breakdown. I just need to time to sort things out.

Kim- What do you need to sort out? Just say it, tell me.

Michael- Kim what I am going to say, I just do not know how to say it.

Kim- Just say it.

Michael- (pauses for what seems like another twenty-seconds) I love you very much Kim, don't you ever forget that. I will always love you. You are the only woman I have ever loved.

Kim- For Pete's sake Michael, just say it, say it.

Michael- (speaks low) I want out.

Kim- I'm sorry, what did you say?

Michael- I want a divorce.

Kim- (drops her glass of wine and stammers) What did you say?

Michael- There is no other woman I swear on my mother's grave, but I want a divorce. I just need some time to sort some things out.

Kim- (screams) Damn you Michael, damn you. (she begins yelling and screaming) How could you Michael? Who is she? Who the fuck is she? I want to know right now. Who the fuck is the other woman? Do I know her?

Michael tries to console her and she kicks him, he loses his grip she pushes him into the table which knocks over the vase of flowers, there is a huge crash

Kim- (hysterical) Get away from me, don't you ever touch me ever again.

Michael- You need to calm down.

Kim- (still yelling) Calm down my ass! How dare you Michael, how dare you?

The kids hear the screaming, Sasha runs to Brandon's room crying.

Sasha- What's going on Brandon? Something is going on downstairs.

Brandon- Mom and Dad are just having a disagreement.

Sasha- No Brandon, I heard a glass or something break, then I heard mom screaming, she is screaming now, what is going on?

Brandon- (hugs her) Shhh! It's going to be okay. It's just an argument.

Sasha- (she looks at him) Are you sure?

Brandon- (knows that it is more than a serious argument, they can hear Kim and Michael screaming) Positive, you can trust me. Do you trust me?

Sasha- Yes I do.

Brandon- Now I want you to put on these headphones.

Sasha- Why?

Brandon- Do you trust me?

Sasha- Yes.

Brandon- Just put them on and listen to some music, it's very relaxing and it will help you sleep. I promise when you get finished, you will feel better and Mom and Dad will have stopped arguing.

> Sasha listens to the music, while Brandon listens
> to what is going on downstairs.

Michael- Please lower your voice, you are going to wake the kids up.

Kim- Fuck waking up the kids, I want them to hear that you are leaving me. How can you do this to me? You should have thought about the kids before you went cheating on me.

Michael- I have never cheated on you and I am not cheating now. I just want a divorce.

Kim- What kind of a man comes home to his wife and says I want a divorce after 15 years of marriage and does not give her a fucking explanation? Tell me what kind of a man does that? I'll tell you the kind of man who does, a man who has been cheating on his wife and now he wants to leave her for the other woman, but I will not allow it.

> Brandon hears this and puts his hands to his
> mouth, the tears comes to eyes.

Kim- I hate you, Michael. I hate you.

Michael- I love you Kim more than you will ever know. I can't explain this but it has nothing to do with another woman. Please, you have to trust me.

Kim- (crying) Then why? Why Michael. Tell me why? I need to know why??

Michael- I really do not have an answer. I just want a divorce. I just don't want to be married; I just want to be by myself and in my own space. I know that you may not understand this right now and it's probably not making any sense. But I do not mean to hurt you.

Kim- You must think I am stupid, you must think I am really stupid. Kim grabs a knife from the drawer.

Michael- So what, you want to kill me?

Brandon is hearing everything.

Kim- Yes, I want to kill you because if I can't have you, no other bitch will. (she walks towards Michael waving the knife in his face)

Michael walks backwards.

Michael- Kim please calm down I am not leaving you for another woman. You can have everything, the house, the cars, I will continue to pay the mortgage, the car notes, the kids school fees, and I don't want to make this harder than it already is.

Kim- Fuck you Michael. (she moves closer and tries to stab him, Michaels tries to grab the knife out of her hands) Get off of me you Bastard, get off. (Michael pulls the knife away from her) So what, you don't think I can grab another knife? Kim reaches in to the draw and gets another knife.

Michael- Kim, please be careful and think about this.

Kim- Did you think about this before you came home and said you want a divorce? You are not leaving me, not alive. I would rather kill you and go to jail than have you leave me.

Michael- Kim calm down, Baby please. You are talking crazy.

Kim crying, runs towards him with the knife, Michael grabs the knife but this time Kim did manage to stab him in the arm.

Michael- Shit, I can't believe you stabbed me.

Kim- 15 years and two kids, we just celebrated our anniversary and you come to me with some bullshit like this, you must have lost your mind, you must not know about me.

Michael- It's not about you, it's about me.

Kim- Easy for you so say that Michael. I can't live without you, do you know that? What about the kids? Did your black ass think about that? You don't think that they need their dad? What the fuck are they supposed to do?

Michael- I will always be here. I will always be there for you all.

Kim- What the fuck are you talking about? I want you here in the house we bought, and where all the memories are. (Kim begins to cry) I swear Michael, I love you more than life. If you leave me I am going to die of a broken heart, my heart is hurting right now. How can you leave me, why? Why? What have I done? Tell me Michael what have I done?

> She rushes towards him again with a knife; Michael grabs the knife but in the process gets stabbed in the knee. And they knock down a plant stand.

Michael- Aah Kim, are you crazy?

Kim-Who is she?

> Michael is bleeding.

Michael- There is no other woman. I just need to sort some things out. It's not about you, it's me. I can't believe you stabbed me in the leg. I am fucking bleeding.

Kim- I don't care. I cannot believe that you are leaving me for some bitch, who is she Michael? It will be so much better if you tell me who she is.

Michael- Kim, I think I am having a nervous breakdown. I have been going to a shrink. It's not about you.

Kim- (crying and screaming) I want you out of my house. I want you out now. Go to your bitch. You had better leave right now or else.

Michael- Or else what?

Kim- There is no telling what I will do to you if you stay here tonight.

Michael- You are psycho, you know that?

Kim- I swear Michael, I will kill you.

> Brandon knows he has to do something before things get worse he comes running downstairs yelling.

Brandon- Mom! Dad! Are you two okay?

Kim- Hi Honey, how are you?

Brandon- You tell me, I heard noise and screams and just wanted to make sure you were alright.

Michael- Oh it's nothing Son, your mom and I are just talking.

Kim- How long have you been up?

Brandon- I've been up for a while.

Kim- Oh okay.

> Brandon looks down at the floor, he sees broken glass and he sees the broken vase and the flowers on the floor.

Brandon- What happened there?

Kim- Oh silly me, your dad was tickling me and I dropped my glass, silly me.

Brandon - Are you all coming up to bed?

Kim- In a minute Brandon.

Brandon- Dad, I want to show you something it's very important, please come with me now.

Michael- Not right now Son, give me a few minutes.

Brandon- No I need to show this to you right now, it cannot wait.

Michael- Okay, (he looks at Kim and says) See you upstairs, Honey.

Kim- (nods) Sure.

Michael- So what do you want to show me?

Brandon- Come up to my room, Dad.

Michael- Okay.

Michael- So what is going on?

Brandon- You tell me, Dad.

Michael- Oh nothing, just tired.

Brandon- Dad, I heard everything. I know that you want a divorce from Mom and I know Mom is angry. You can sleep in my room tonight just to be safe.

> Michael is shocked, he does not know whether to hug Brandon or cry.

Michael- Son, I am so sorry.

Brandon- Dad, it's okay. Dad, you are bleeding.

Michael- I know but it's nothing a band aid can't fix. Brandon, despite what you heard, I am not leaving her for another woman. You have to believe me.

Brandon- I believe you Dad. You do not have to explain anything to me, I just don't want Mom to do anything stupid so I think you should sleep in my room tonight.

Michael- How do you plan on telling that to your mom?

Brandon- Trust me, let me handle this.

Michael- Hey I am not going to say no, I do not know what frame of mind your mom is in.

Brandon- Okay let me go and talk to Mom.

> Brandon goes over to his parents' room, Kim is lying in the bed crying, she sees Brandon and tries to wipe her eyes really fast.

Kim- Son, why aren't you sleeping?

Brandon- I can't sleep.

Kim- Boy you had better get your butt in bed.

Brandon- Mom, it's okay to cry.

Kim- Honey, what are you talking about? I am not crying.

Brandon- Mom, it's okay. I know.

Kim- Know what?

Brandon- Mom, I heard everything. I heard you and Dad arguing and I know that he wants a divorce.

Kim- (hugs him) Oh Brandon, I am so sorry.

Brandon- Mom, it's okay. I am sorry Dad feels that way. But I don't want you to do anything stupid, so I am going to have Dad sleep in my room, are you going to be okay?

Kim- (begins to cry) Oh Brandon. I can't believe your dad wants to leave us.

Brandon- (hugs her, they are tears in his eyes as well) It's okay, Mom. Do you want me to sleep with you tonight while Dad sleeps in the other room?

Kim- Oh no, no Son you do not have to. I'm a grown woman. I am going to be okay.

Brandon- I know, but I want to.

Kim- Honey, that is not necessary, trust me I'm okay.

Brandon- Are you sure?

Kim- Of course, thanks for asking.

Brandon- (hugs her) Love you, Mom.

Kim- Love you too. Now go to bed and get your rest.

Brandon- Okay, see you in the morning.

> Brandon walks back to his room, where his dad is.

Michael- How did it go?

Brandon- It went well. I am going to check in with her later. You can sleep with me, Dad. Look, I brought your pajamas.

Michael- You are the best.

Brandon- I learned from the best.

> They hug each other. It's two o'clock in the morning and Brandon gets up to go and check on Kim. She has been crying all night. Brandon walks into the room. He hears her crying.

Brandon- Mom, Mom, are you okay?

Kim- I am fine Brandon, why aren't you sleeping? It's a school night.

Brandon - I know but I wanted to check on you.

Kim- (tries to smile) That is so sweet but I am okay.

Brandon- No you are not, Mom; I heard you crying all night. Have you been able to sleep?

Kim- No, but I am going to be okay.

Brandon- Do you remember what you told me when I cried a lot?

Kim- Yes I do, Son.

Brandon- Okay then I am going to tell you the same thing. Mom, you are going to make yourself sick crying like that.

Kim-You know that you are too mature for your age.

Brandon- Now I am going to lie down here with you and I am not taking no for an answer.

Kim- Honey, you really do not have to do this.

Brandon- I know Mom, but I want to.

> He jumps into bed with her and hugs her. They
> fall asleep together.

Scene 17

It's the next morning Michael is fixing breakfast; Kim is still lying in bed. Brandon goes and checks in on her.

Brandon- Mom, are you okay? Would you like some breakfast?

Kim- No, I am not hungry.

Brandon- Dad is going to take us to school.

Kim- No! No! I do not want him to.

Brandon- Mom, it's okay. Just lie down and get some rest.

Kim- I guess. But I will pick you both up from school.

Brandon- Okay.

> Brandon goes downstairs, Sasha is in the kitchen talking with her dad.

Sasha- Dad, where is Mom?

Michael- She is lying down; she is not feeling too well. Actually I need to go and check on her. I will be right back.

> Michael goes upstairs and walks into the bed-
> room, he hears Kim crying in bed. He walks
> over and says,

Michael- Good morning.

> Kim does not answer.

Michael- Kim, I know that you are angry with me and you have every right to be, but Kim you have to believe me when I say this. There is no other woman. There will never be another woman. I love you too much for that. I just don't want to be married anymore. I know that it does not make sense to you, but you have to believe me.

> Brandon is standing by the door and he is hearing
> everything. Kim does not answer.

Michael- Please say something Honey, are you okay?

> Kim does not answer. Michael walks closer to
> her and he can see the tears flowing down her
> face, he gets teary eyed just seeing her so sad, he
> wipes the tears from off of her face

Kim- (crying) Please leave, Michael. Don't touch me.

Michael- I am so sorry Kim, I never meant to hurt you. This is just something I want, and it may be selfish of me but I just want out and it has nothing to do with you at all. It's me. Please try to understand, Honey please try. The reason why I have been late is because I was going to counseling. I feel like I am having a nervous breakdown Kim. I just don't know.

> Kim keeps on crying.

Michael- Honey, please stop crying. I made breakfast. Are you hungry?

> Kim does not respond, she just keeps on crying.

Michael- What can I do or say Kim, to make this better?

> Kim does not respond. Michael looks at her for ten seconds she turns her back in the opposite direction still lying on the bed.

Kim- Michael, please leave. I do not want to be bothered.

Michael- I understand. (he leaves the room)

Michael- (heads downstairs and says to the kids) Are you all ready?

Sasha- Yes. Is Mom okay?

Michael- Yes, she is going to be fine. Okay, let's go.

Brandon- Let me just check on her quickly before we go, is that okay Dad.

Michael- Sure.

> Kim is still lying in bed crying. Brandon walks over and hugs her.

Brandon- Mom, I love you so much. It hurts me to see you hurting.

Kim- Oh Son, I love you so much. I am going to be okay. Don't worry about me. I just have a broken heart.

Brandon- What can I do to mend your broken heart?

Kim- (cries) Only your dad can take care of that Brandon. Oh it hurts so bad.

Brandon consoles her and has tears in his eyes.

Brandon- I am so sorry, Mom. I really am.

Kim- Look I want you to go to school. I will be fine.

Brandon- Okay, love you.

Kim- I love you more.

Brandon (heads downstairs) I am ready, Dad.

Michael pulls up at the school, everyone gets out of the car.

Sasha- Daddy, are you picking us up?

Michael- Yes.

Sasha gives him a hug and runs off to meet up with her friends.
Brandon gets out of the car he looks very sad, Michael hugs him.

Michael- Son, are you okay?

Brandon- No, but I will be okay.

Michael- I am so sorry. I never meant to hurt your mom.

Brandon- (with tears in his eyes) Why, Dad? Why?

Michael- (with tears in his eyes) I just want out and it has nothing to do with you, another woman or your mom. I think I am having a nervous breakdown or going through some middle age crisis. I am getting counseling for it. I just need to sort some things out.

Brandon- What things?

Michael- It's so complicated, you would not understand.

Brandon- I have to get going. See you later.

Michael- I don't get a hug?

Brandon- Of course.

> They hug each other.
> Michael walks to his car; he gets inside and just sits there. The song by Roberta Flack comes on, *The First Time Ever I Saw Your Face*. The tears run down his face as he reminisces about the first time he met Kim at college, she was a college freshman attending freshman orientation. He was a college sophomore. The day Brandon was born, he is just reminiscing.
> There is a tap on the passenger side of his car, Michael jumps out of his daydream it's a cop. Michel winds down his window down.

Michael- Officer, is there a problem?

Officer- That is what I want to ask you; you have been parked here for half an hour, are you okay? This is not a parking zone.

Michael- My apologies, I will move my car.

Officer- Okay.

> The officer walks away and Michael drives back to the house.
> Kim is on the phone with her mother telling her everything.

Stephanie- He did what? You know I am not surprised. That asshole. He is a dead man you hear me, when your dad finds out. Oh it's over.

Kim- Mom, can you calm down please?

Stephanie- That bastard comes home and says he is leaving you for another woman after 15 years and you want me to calm down. I am texting your dad right now. He is a dead man. What about my babies, how are they doing with all this bullshit?

Kim- They are fine. Brandon knows, but Sasha does not.

Stephanie- Well who is the bitch that he is leaving you for?

Kim- Mom, I do not know, he said he is not leaving me for another woman he just wants out.

Stephanie- He can't even be man enough and tell you the truth, he is a pussy. Where is he now?

Kim- He went to drop the kids off to school.

Stephanie- Honey, how are you holding up? Do you need me to come over? I am on my way.

Kim- Can I answer you first? Dag, Mom. No I do not want you over here right now. I can handle this.

Stephanie- Are you sure?

Kim- Yes Mom, just chill.

Stephanie- Just chill, I have been waiting for his black ass to screw up, oh I have been waiting for it. You know I never liked him for you. Your dad and I were against this union from the get go. He was never good enough for you. I'm glad it's over.

Kim- Well thanks Mom, like I really need to be hearing this right now.

Stephanie's cell rings.

Stephanie- Honey, this is your dad calling. I just texted him and he is calling me back. We will talk later.

Kim- Okay.

Stephanie answers her cell.

Stephanie- Hello.

Teddy- What the hell is going on? Did I read your text correct?

Stephanie- You sure did. Michael is leaving our daughter for another woman.

Teddy- What? Are you positive about that Stephanie?

Stephanie- Yes, of course. Where are you?

Teddy- I am in my car, on my way home. I am going to kill that son of a bitch. Where are the kids?

Stephanie- At school.

Teddy- Do the kids know?

Stephanie- Brandon knows.

Teddy- Well, who is the other woman?

Stephanie- He said there is no other woman. He just wants out of the marriage.

Teddy- What! What kind of shit is that? Take my gun out of the closet Stephanie.

Stephanie- Okay, see you soon.

Scene 18

Kim goes to take a shower; Michael pulls up at the house, he calls out to Kim.

Michael- Kim, I'm back. We need to talk.

> He then walks upstairs to the bedroom and sees that Kim is in the shower. He begins to pack a bag. Kim comes out of the shower with a robe on.

Kim- I see you are packing to go to her house. I bet she cannot wait for you to leave me.

Michael- What are you talking about? There is no other woman. Please believe me on that.

Kim- I do not care what you say, there is another woman.

Michael- Fine, believe what you want.

Kim- How could you, Michael? How could you hurt the kids and me like that?

Michael- That was never my intent. I thought about this for a very long time.

Kim- Oh you did, ha?

Michael- I meant I felt this was the best way. I can't be the husband you married. I have demons that I have to deal with.

Kim- What am I not pretty enough? What did I do? Just tell me and I will fix it.

Michael- It's not you, Kim. It's me. I am the one with the issues. I just don't want to be married anymore. I will still be around for you and the kids.

Kim- You will never see those kids again.

Michael- Please don't fight me on this. They are my kids too and I want to be a part of their lives.

Kim- You did this not me. You could see your kids every day, but you chose not to. You chose to leave us here, and now you want to see them everyday. Just how did you plan on managing that, ha?

Michael- If you would just work with me, Kim. Please, I do not want a messy divorce.

Kim- You should have thought about that before you cheated on me.

Michael- I never cheated on you and I am not cheating now. Look I am staying at the Hilton hotel. Room 942 if you need to call me.

Kim- Just leave my house.

Michael- This is our house. And I am not leaving until the kids get home. I am picking them up from school.

Kim- No, you are not.

Michael- Kim, I promised them that I would.

Kim- Well you are not good at keeping promises these days. You promised to stay with me through thick and thin until death do us part. But you are leaving me so they will understand.

Michael- Kim Honey, this is not necessary.

The phone rings and Kim answers.

Kim- Hello.

School Counselor- Is this Mrs. Stevenson?

Kim- Yes.

School Counselor- We will be letting the kids out two hours early because there is a leak and water everywhere. So the kids are going to be ready in an hour.

Kim- Okay, thank you. I will be there.

Michael- Who was it?

Kim- The school. The kids are being let out early because of a water leak.

Michael- Great, I will go and get them.

Kim- No, Michael.

The door bell rings.

Kim- Who the hell is it?

Kim runs downstairs to get the door, she looks out the peep hole and it's her parents.

Kim- Oh, Lord have mercy.

She opens the door

Teddy- Honey, are you okay?

Kim- Yes, Dad.

Teddy- Where is he? Where is that bastard?

Kim- Dad, please calm down.

Teddy- I said where is he?

Kim- He is upstairs.

Kim- What is going on? (she looks at her mom) Mom, what did you say to Dad?

Stephanie- Everything you told me.

Kim- Look I need to leave soon to pick up the kids; I do not want any drama while I am gone.

Stephanie- I cannot make any promises.

> Teddy runs up the stairs to Kim's room. He sees Michael, he rushes at him to choke him, and he grabs Michael.

Michael- Get your hands off of me. (Michael pushes Teddy off of him) Have you lost your mind?

Teddy- No, but apparently you have. So you want to leave my daughter, ha. I knew you were a loser from the start.

Michael- I don't have time for this. I have somewhere to go.

Teddy- Oh really. (Teddy pulls out a 45 mm gun.) Oh I have been waiting for the opportunity to use this on you, yes I have. Do you remember what I told you privately on the day of your wedding?

Michael- (startled) No, and you better put that gun away.

> Teddy pulls the trigger back you can hear the clicking sound.

Teddy- You don't, ha? Well let me refresh your memory. I told you if you hurt my daughter in any way I was going to kill you. Do you remember that now?

Michael- Get out of my house.

> Teddy pulls the trigger and shoots at Michael, Michael ducks and the bullet misses his head by an inch. Michael looks shocked and scared at the same time he cannot believe Kim's dad shot at him. Kim and Stephanie hear the shot and run upstairs.

Teddy- (pointing the gun at Michael) Now that was just a warning to let you know that I am serious. Do you hear me?

Michael- (shocked) Yes.

> Kim and Stephanie run into the room and Kim sees her dad with the gun pointing it at Michael.

Kim- Dad! What are you doing? Please put the gun down. This is crazy.

Stephanie- Yes Honey, I do not want to lose you. If you kill this man you are going to go to jail. Think, Teddy.

Kim- I do not want you to kill him Daddy, please put the gun down.

> Teddy is still pointing the gun.

Teddy- You see how lucky you are? I would have killed you dead, you hear me? But they are right, you are not worth it. Now get out.

Michael stands there for what seems like five minutes, you can see the hurt, anger and pain in his eyes and face. He gets teary eyed. He looks at his wife, then her mother then Teddy, then he walks out.
Kim begins to cry and hold her heart, her mom consoles her.

Stephanie- Its okay Honey, its okay. We are going to help you through this.

Kim- (Yells out to Michael) Where are you going?

Michael- I am going to pick up my kids from school. I will return them to you and then I will leave.

SCENE 19

10 YEARS LATER

Michael has sold his law firm, however he does consulting on the side. He still lives in California, but he recently moved to Santa Barbara. He sees the kids on the weekends. Kim has never recovered from her broken heart, she is in and out of the hospital, she has lost a lot of weight, she still cries every night. Brandon actually does all the cooking and cleaning because Kim is too weak or spaced out to do anything sometimes. She now drinks and gets delirious at times. It hurts Brandon to see his mom so sad and his dad so happy. He helps his sister with her homework, does the laundry, makes breakfast, and takes care of his mother. Kim is sitting outside in her huge backyard staring at the large pool that overlooks Beverly Hills. Kim is looking into space with glass of Vodka in her hands. Brandon walks up to her.

Brandon- Hey Mom, I have done the laundry. Can I get you anything? Would you like a sandwich? You have not eaten anything all day.

> Kim is still staring into space, she does not respond.

Brandon- Mom, did you hear me?

> Kim does not respond, he walks closer and taps her.

Brandon- Mom, are you okay?

Kim- Yes, what is going on?

Brandon- Did you not hear me earlier?

Kim- No what? What did you say?

Brandon- (sad) Nothing, Mom. Do you want something to eat?

Kim- No Honey, I am good.

Brandon- Mom, you are really thin and you need to eat, I will make you a sandwich.

Kim- Brandon, tell your dad he needs to mow the lawn, the grass is awfully high. Actually tell him to come downstairs and cut the grass now.

> Brandon looks at her with a sad face.

Kim- He is probably still upstairs on the computer. That is all he does is stay on that computer. Why are you sill standing here? Tell him to come downstairs now.

Brandon- I can't.

Kim- What do you mean you can't?

Brandon- Mom, Dad does not live here remember? He left years ago.

> Kim slowly, sips on her drink and begins to cry,
> Brandon consoles her.

Brandon- Don't cry Mom, it's going to be okay. Did you take your medication?

Kim- To hell with that. Everyone thinks I am losing my mind so I don't need that.

Brandon- Mom, you are suffering from depression, you need to take them and please stop drinking.

Kim- You had better watch your tone, Boy. I am your mother.

Brandon- Yes, sorry Mom. I am going to fix you a sandwich.

Kim- Good, you do that.

> Brandon walks into the kitchen to fix the sand-
> wich. Sasha is on the couch doing her home-
> work. Brandon walks over to her.

Brandon- How is it going Sasha?

Sasha- I need help with my homework. Mom or Dad used to help me and now they are not around. (Sasha begins to cry even more)

Brandon- I will help you with your homework just give me a few minutes. I need to fix Mom a sandwich.

Sasha- I miss Dad, I want things to be how they used to be.

Brandon- We all do Sasha.

Sasha- What is wrong with Mom, Brandon?

Brandon- Oh nothing, she just misses Dad very much. It hurts her so bad that she sometimes drinks to hide the pain.

Sasha- So now you are taking the role of Mommy and Daddy?

Brandon- (laughs) I can never take the role of Mom nor Dad, but in their absence I will do my very best.

Sasha- I love you Brandon, you are the best big brother. You are taking care of everyone, who is taking care of you?

Brandon- I can take care of myself.

Sasha- When you go away to college what is going to happen to Mom and me? I am going to miss you.

Brandon- Remember Grandma and Grandpa are going to move in here to help you and Mom out okay. Everything is going to be fine.

> They hear a scream from Kim outside, Brandon runs outside to see what is going on

Sasha- What is going on?

Brandon- You stay here and I will go and check on Mom.

> Brandon runs outside, and Kim is on the floor holding her heart crying. Brandon is scared.

Brandon- Mom! Mom! Are you okay.

Kim- My heart hurts, my heart is broken. I want my husband back. (she begins to cry louder) Oh Lord, oh God why?

> Brandon picks her up and brings her inside, Kim is still holding her heart. He puts her on the couch.

Brandon- Mom, it's going to be okay, I am going to call your personal doctor and have him come over right now.

Brandon gets on the phone and calls Dr. Fenham.

Dr. Fenham- Hello.

Brandon- Hi, its Brandon, my mom collapsed outside. Can you come over right now?

Dr. Fenham- Absolutely, I will be there in thirty minutes. Where is she now?

Brandon- I have her on the couch.

Dr. Fenham- Is she conscious?

Brandon- Yes. Please hurry

Dr. Fenham- I am on my way.

Brandon walks over to his mom on the couch, he wipes her face with a towel because she is sweating.

Brandon- Mom, are you okay?

Kim- I just want to die, I just want to die.

Brandon- Mom, you have us to live for, you don't need Dad. It's going to be okay, the doctor is on his way over.

Kim- I'm sorry I did not meant to say that.

Brandon- It's okay, Mom.

The door bell rings and it's Dr. Fenham.

Brandon- Hello Dr. Fenham, how are you?

Dr. Fenham- I am doing great, how is your mom?

Brandon- I don't know.

Dr. Fenham- Where is she?

Brandon- She is in the living room on the couch.

They both walk over to her.

Dr. Fenham- Mrs. Stevenson, how are you doing?

Kim- Fine, why are you here?

Dr. Fenham- I am here to check up on you.

Kim- I am okay.

Dr. Fenham- Have you eaten today?

Kim- No, not really. I am not hungry.

Dr. Fenham- Ms. Stevenson, you have to eat.

Brandon- She hasn't eaten all day. (his voice breaks) I gave her fruit earlier this morning and I fixed her a sandwich this afternoon.

Dr. Fenham- Kim, it's imperative that you eat. You need to eat, and you need to take the medication. If you do not you will have to be hospitalized, is that what you want Ms. Stevenson?

Kim- (begins to cry) No. I just want my husband back. Go and get him. Why did he leave me? Why?

Brandon and Dr. Fenham walk away for a moment to talk.

Dr, Fenham- Son, I am worried about you; this is so much for you to take on. Is your mom this way all the time?

Brandon- Yes, for the most part. I don't know what to do. I made breakfast for her, but all she ate was fruit.

Dr. Fenham- She needs to eat Son, your mom is suffering from severe depression and if she does not eat and take the medication, she is going to die. Are you in contact with your father?

Brandon- Yes.

Dr. Fenham- Does he know what is going with her?

Brandon- No, she does not want us to tell him anything.

Dr. Fenham- Does he ask about her?

Brandon- Yes, all the time.

Brandon- What do you say?

Michael- I say she is doing fine.

Dr. Fenham- Is there any chance of reconciliation?

Brandon- No. My dad has moved on, actually he is getting married next weekend.

Dr. Fenham- I see.

Brandon- What is going to happen to my mom doctor?

Dr. Fenham- Well, your parents and I go back a long way. And I am going to do my best to make your mom better, but she has to do her part. If not, I will have to commit her to a treatment center, where she will be under supervision twenty four seven. However, if she eats and takes her medication I would not need to do this. Your mom is extremely sick. She is truly suffering from a broken heart and she is severely depressed.

The tears rolls down Brandon face.

Dr. Fenham- (hugs him) It's going to be okay, who can you call?

Brandon- My grandparents.

Dr. Fenham- You cannot do this by yourself. Can you call them right now and have them come over?

Brandon- Okay.

Brandon gets on the phone and makes the call.

Stephanie- Hello.

Brandon- Hello, Grandma

Stephanie- Hi Honey, is everything okay? How is your mom?

Brandon- She is not doing too well, can you come over?

Stephanie- We are on our way.

Stephanie and Teddy come over, Stephanie runs up to the house. She does not even ring the door bell she uses her keys. She runs into the house screaming.

Stephanie- What is going on with my daughter? What is wrong with her? It's all Michael's fault, I could kill him for what he did to my daughter. I hate him. That bastard.

Teddy and Stephanie walk into the living room and see Kim lying on the couch.

Dr. Fehham- I need to have a word with you both

The three of them leave to talk in the family room .

Dr. Fenham- Your daughter is suffering from severe depression; she is also developing an eating disorder that makes her weak and delirious. I am going to leave her some stronger medication and I am going to keep a close watch on her. I am going to send over a nutritionist to monitor her. If she does not improve in a week I am going to have to admit her.

Stephanie- He did this to her. He did it.

Dr. Fenham- So we are going to give it a week and see what happens.

Teddy- Okay.

> They walk back into the living room look on the couch and Kim is not there.

Teddy- Where did she go? We've only been gone fifteen minutes.

> They walk into the kitchen and sees Kim cooking. Stephanie walks over to her.

Stephanie- Kim Honey, are you okay?

Kim- Of course, what kind of a question is that?

Stephanie- Just asking.

Kim- I am preparing dinner, you all please stay.

Teddy- Sure of course we will, do you need some help, Honey?

Kim- As a matter of fact yes, one of you can slice the tomatoes and the other can make the salad.

> Kim looks at Dr. Fenham and says,

Kim- See, I am doing okay. Aren't you proud of me?

Dr. Fehnham- Yes, I am very pleased.

Kim- So stay for dinner.

Dr. Fenham- I would love to but I have another patient to see. I will take a rain check.

Kim- Okay.

Stephanie walks him to the door.

Stephanie- She seems fine now, how weird is that?

Dr. Fenham- Yeah for how long, though? Please make sure she eats and take the medication. I will check in later to see how things are going. But if things do not improve, I will have to admit her.

Stephanie- She will improve doctor. I will make sure of it.

Dr. Fenham- I hope so. Take care

Stephanie- Bye bye.

Stephanie goes back into the kitchen to help out.

Teddy- So Honey, what are you making?

Kim- Chicken Parmesan.

Stephanie- Hmm, my favorite.

Teddy- So Honey, how are things going?

Kim- Oh just fine. Things could not be better.

Teddy- Have you heard from Michael?

Kim-Michael who?

Teddy- Your ex husband.

Kim- He calls but I do not take nor do I return his calls. Can one of you let the kids know that dinner is ready.

Teddy- I will.

Teddy goes upstairs and Brandon and Sasha are talking.

Teddy- Hi, Kids.

Sasha runs and hugs him.

Sasha- Hi,Grandpa.

Teddy- Are you okay, Sweetie?

Sasah- No. I miss my dad and I want my mom to get better.

Teddy- Your mom is going to be okay. Actually she made us dinner so let's go and eat.

Sasha- Oh good.

Sasha runs out of the room. Teddy walks over to Brandon.

Teddy- Are you okay?

Brandon- Yes.

Teddy- You know your mom really appreciates you taking care of her like that.

Brandon- She took care of us from birth so it's the least I can do for her.

Teddy- Let's go and have some of her delicious food.

Brandon- Sounds good to me.

Scene 20

It's eight years later and Michael is getting married, he asked Brandon to be the best man but he declined. Michael is extremely excited, he is getting married to someone he met in law school some thirty years ago, her name is Carlotta Thompson. Carlotta has never been married; she is a lawyer. Carlotta had a crush on Michael back in law school. The chapel is full with at least 200 people. Carlotta's sister and mom are putting the finishing touches on her.

Her mom- Honey, you look beautiful, I am so happy for you. You deserve the best.

Her sister- You do. And I am so glad you are finally getting married at 52.

    (they both laugh)

Carlotta- Better late than never. In my forty seven years I never met a man worth marrying other than Michael. He has gone through so much in the past ten years.

Sister- How is his family doing?

Carlotta- According to Brandon, they are doing fine. The kids are so sweet and very mannerly.

Sister- Where are Brandon and Sasha?

Carlotta- I hope they make it to the reception. I asked Sasha if she wanted to be in the wedding and she said no. Michael asked Brandon to be his best man and he said no. (Carlotta begins to cry her sister grabs a tissue and consoles her)

Sister- Carlotta, it's okay.

Carlotta- I think they hate me, I think they believe I took their father away from them. If only Brandon and Sasha knew how much he loves them and their mom. I wish they knew. When Brandon told Michael he did not want to be his best man, Michael broke down and cried; he was deeply hurt. He loves his kids so much, I love them too, but I know it's a sensitive situation so I stay out of it. I just want them to know that I will not stand in the way of them being with their father. He is such a good man Kimmie, he really is. I feel so lucky to have found him.

Kimmie- Look, today is your day. You are a good person and you deserve this. We are so happy for you and Michael.

> Michael pops his head in the room, Carlotta tries
> to hide herself.

Carlotta- Don't you know its bad luck to see the bride before the ceremony?

Kimmie- Hi Michael, I am going to leave you two lovebirds. See you all later.

Michael- See you later, Kimmie.

Carlotta- (hugs her sister Kimmie) I love you.

Kimmie- Love you more.

Michael grabs Carlotta's face gently and says,

Michael- I love you Carlotta and it's okay to marry me. You are not hurting anyone by doing this. You deserve happiness, we both do. I love you. It is not bad luck seeing you before the wedding; we are going to get married, regardless. I love the fact that you do not judge anyone. You accept everyone for who they are. You are so good to me and my kids. Your heart is so pure. I love you. I can't wait to make you my wife.

Carlotta begins to cry, Michael wipes the tears from her eyes, they embrace, and Carlotta's mom walks in.

Mom- Hello Michael, how are you?

Michael- (hugs her) I am fine Mrs. Thompson.

Mom- I just wanted to let you know that they are looking for you, the service is getting ready to start.

Michael- Okay. (he kisses Carlotta and says) I love you, see in a few. (he then kisses her mom) See you out there.

Mom- You too, Son.

Carlotta- This is the happiest day of my life.

Mom- Good, I am so happy for you. I love you Carlotta.

Carlotta- Love you too, Mom. See you outside in a few.

Carlotta's dad walks in.

Carlotta- Dad. (She hugs him)

Dad- You look beautiful.

Carlotta- I am so nervous and happy at the same time.

Dad- You are going to be fine. Let's go, they are waiting for us.

The music begins to play and the flower girls walk out, then the ring bearer, then the bridesmaid. Then everyone stands as the song, *Here Comes the Bride*, begins to play. Carlotta is being escorted by her father; she is wearing a white lace bodice dress with a very long train and a cute veil. They walk up to the altar.

Pastor Riches- Who gives this woman to be married?

Mr. & Mrs. Thompson- We do.

They both kiss Carlotta and take their seats, Michael grabs her hands.

Pastor Riches- We are gathered here today to witness the union of Carlotta Ann Thompson and Michael Roy Stevenson. What the Lord has put together let no other put asunder. If there is anyone here who sees fit why these two should not get married, speak now or forever hold your peace.

Nothing but silence.

Pastor Riches- Good, lets move on. Both Carolotta and Michael have written their own vows so Carlotta please read yours.

Michael and Carlotta hold hands as they face each other. Carlotta begins to read her vows to Michael.

Carlotta- Michael you are the best thing that has ever happened to me. I love you more than life. I am so glad our paths crossed again. You are the wind beneath my wings and I am so grateful to have you in my life.

Pastor Riches- Please repeat after me Carlotta.

Pastor Riches- With this ring I thee wed.

Carlotta- With this ring I thee wed.

Pastor Riches- (says to Michael) It's your turn.

Michael- Carlotta you came into my life when I least expected it; you make my cloudy days bright and my long days short. You are the apple of my eye, when I see you I see paradise. You are my everything and I am happiest when I am with you. You are the breath that I breathe and the love of my life.

> Michael takes the ring from the ring bearer; he places the ring on Carlotta's finger.

Pastor Riches- Okay put the ring on her finger and repeat after me. With this ring I thee wed.

Michael- With this ring I thee wed.

> Before the pastor pronounced Michael and Carlotta husband and wife, three shots were fired from the roof of the church; two hit Michael in his chest, he lies dying on the altar. Everyone started screaming and running out of the church. Carlotta and the pastor hold Michael, and he falls to the ground.

Carlotta- (holding Michael with blood on her hands and dress, she screams) Why? Why? Someone call 911 please, someone do something.

Pastor Riches- (grabs the mike asking) Is there a doctor in the house? Is there a doctor here?

> Carlotta's parents are crying in shock. Carlotta's sister runs to the altar to help her. Carlotta's

brother runs outside to look at the roof to find the
gunman, but no one was there. Michael lies on
the floor bleeding to death.

Carlotta- (holding him says) Please don't leave me Michael.
Please don't leave me. I hope it's not my fault you got shot. If
so I would have just remained your friend.

Michael tries to talk.

Carlotta- Please don't try to talk Honey, save your energy for
later, you need your energy.

Michael- I love you Carlotta, my will is in my safe.

Carlota- Honey, shhh! As she strokes his head.

Michael- (gasping for air and tries to talk to Carlotta) Please
listen, the will is in my safe and the keys are in my gold box in
my closet.

Carlotta- (crying) Don't leave me Michael, please don't leave
me, I have a surprise for you.

Michael dies in her arms.

Carlotta- (cries) Oh God no, no! No, Michael you can't leave
me, oh God the surprise is I am pregnant with your son. (she is
sobbing and is all choked up) I am three months pregnant.

Carlotta lies on Michael, her sister tries to re-
move her but she would not move.

Kimmie- Its okay Carlotta, we are here for you, we are going to
help you through this.

Carlotta- I don't want to leave. I just want to stay here.

Kimmie- Honey, you can't.

Carlotta- Pastor continue please.

Pastor Riches- Well yes. By the power invested in me I now pronounce you man and wife.

Carlotta- (kisses Michael) I love you Michael. I love you.

> Her brothers pull her up from Michael, she is sobbing.

Carlotta- Please, I want to stay with him, he is my husband.

Carlotta's brother- Honey, I know you are hurting but the ambulance is here, they need to take him.

Carlotta- Just give me five more minutes. Please just five more minutes.

> You can hear the ambulance sirens and the police sirens in the background; it's a nightmare. The news hits the airwaves like a tornado. Michael's best friend Ron is at an airport and sees the news and breaks down crying.

Ron- I can't believe this shit.

Lady at the airport- Did you know him?

Ron- Yes, he was my best friend.

Lady- He was my lawyer several years ago and he helped me win a case. I am so sorry to hear that. Who would do such a thing?

Ron- It's a crazy world.

Lady- Please give his family my condolences. I was an old client and he was good to me and really helped me.

Ron- I will.

Scene 21

Stephanie sees the news and calls Kim, Brandon answers.

Brandon- Hello, Grandma

Stephanie- Where is your Mom?

Brandon- Downstairs making dinner.

Stephanie- Okay, put her on the phone now it's urgent.

Brandon- Is everything okay?

Stephanie- No, just put your mom on the phone.

Brandon- (takes the phone to Kim who is in the kitchen) It's Grandma and she says it's urgent.

Kim- Hello.

Stephanie- Honey, are you watching the news?

Kim- No, why?

Stephanie- Turn on the news now.

Kim- Why? What is going on, Mom?

Stephanie- Michael was shot and killed at his wedding.

> Kim drops the phone and screams.

Stephanie- Kim, Kim! Kim, are you okay?

> Stephanie hangs up the phone, grabs her car keys
> and heads to Kim's house.
> Kim runs and turns the TV on and sees for her-
> self.

Reporter- Well known retired lawyer (his picture is being shown) Michael Stevenson was murdered at his wedding this afternoon; three shots were fired from the roof of the church building piecing Mr. Stevenson in his chest. He died at the church in the arms of his bride, Carlotta Thompson. What a tragedy, police are still trying to find out who killed the well known lawyer on his wedding day. Right now there are no suspects.

> Kim screams out oh God no, no God! Oh God!
> She grabs her heart.

Brandon- (rushes over to her) Oh Mom. Oh Mom. (they both begin to cry)

> Sasha is holding her mouth in disbelief, she can-
> not believe it.

Kim- (screaming) Why? Oh God, why? Why did they kill him? Why, God? Why?

Brandon (crying as he tries to console her) It's okay, Mother, it's okay. The police are going to find out who did this.

The doorbell rings and its Stephanie, she is beside herself. Brandon goes to the door.

Stephanie- (hugs him) Brandon, I am so sorry about your father.

Brandon- (hugs her back crying) Thanks, Grandma.

Stephanie- Where is your mom and Sasha?

Brandon- They should be in the living room.

Stephanie walks into the living and Kim is on the floor crying.

Kim- Oh God, why? Oh, Michael! Michael!

Stephanie- (consoles her) It's okay, Honey, it's okay, I am here for you.

Brandon- Where is Sasha?

Brandon goes upstairs to check on Sasha and she is watching the news crying. Brandon goes and hugs her.

Sasha- Why? Who killed our daddy? I want him back. (she continues to cry, Brandon cries as he tries to console)

There is a knock on the door.

Teddy- I wonder who this is. I will get it.

Teddy walks to the front door and opens the door and there are two detectives.

Teddy- How can I help you?

Detective #1- Good Morning, we are here to see Ms. Stevenson.

Teddy- For what?

Detective #2- First of all our condolences to the family. We knew Michael very well and we are sorry about what happened.

Teddy- Come on in.

Kim and Stephanie come to the door.

Kim- What is going on?

Detective #2- This is very hard for us, but we need to ask you some questions.

Kim- My ex husband was just murdered and you all want to ask questions?

Detective #1- Yes we are aware of that, but we have to get this investigation started.

Kim- Do you have to do this now?

Detective #1- Yes.

The detectives, Kim and her parents are sitting in the living room on the couch.

Detective #2- Do you know of anyone who might have wanted him dead?

Kim- No.

Detective #1- You two had a very bitter divorce, correct?

Kim- That is none of your business.

Detective #1- Okay. Did Michael have any enemies? Anyone at all?

Kim- Not that I'm aware of.

Detective #2- Any family members that you know that may have wanted to see him dead or tried to kill him?

Kim- No.

Detective #1- Your next-door neighbor said that they heard shots one time at this house several years back. Is that correct?

Kim- Not sure what my nosey neighbor is talking about.

Detective #2- Thank you again Ms. Stevenson for your time and again, my condolences.

The detectives leave and walk back to their car.

Detective #1- What do you think?

Detective #2- It's too early to say.

Detective #2- What about Michael's current wife?

Detective #1- What about her? She is not really the wife, because he got killed before the pastor announce them husband and wife.

Detective #2- How do you know that? Were you there at the wedding?

Detective #1- Of course not, but it was all over the news.

Detective #2- I think it's someone he knew.

Detective #1- Well that is obvious.

Detective #2- No I meant someone close to him, like family.

Detective #1- No way Man. It could be his line of work. He put a lot of folks away Man, he was well loved and well hated all the same.

Detective #2- That is what I think Man, I could be wrong but I have a gut feeling about it.

Detective #1- We need to talk to Carlotta.

Detective #2- Yeah we need to.

Detective #1- Let's do that now.

Scene 22

A few hours go by and the detectives pull up to Carlotta and Michael's house. It's a huge mansion.

Detective #1- Damn! She is living the life.

Detective #2- Yes, I want that life. Look at all that land.

> They walk up to the mansion and try to ring the doorbell.

Detective #1- Check this out, they don't have a door bell, they have a monitor and an intercom.

Detective #2- Damn.

> Detective #2 hits the intercom. Maid looks at the monitor she sees two cops, she speaks through the intercom.

Maria- How can I help you?

Detective #1- We are here to see Mrs. Stevenson.

Maria- Is she expecting you?

Detective #2- No but we need to talk to her.

Detective #2- (looks at Detective #1 and says) Why did you call her Mrs. Stevenson? She never got married to the man.

Detective #1- Whatever Man, I do not have time for any legality right now. I think it would be rude to call her by any other name. Let's see what she says when we call her that.

She goes to Carlotta and says,

Maid- Two detectives are here to see you.

Carlotta- Okay, let them in.

Maid- Are you sure?

Carlotta- Of course.

Maid- (goes and opens the door) Hello, how are you both doing?

Detective #1- Okay.

Detective #2- Fine thanks.

Maid- Please follow me this way.

The detectives follow the maid down this long hall to the living room.

Maid- Please have a seat. Mrs. Stevenson will be right down.

Carlotta- (walks into the room holding her son in her arms and says) Hello Gentlemen, how can I help you?

Detective #1- Mrs. Stevenson how are you doing?

Carlotta- I am fine.

Detective #2- Great! You have a lovely home.

Carlotta- Thank you.

Carlotta- Can I get you all something? Tea, water, or vodka.

Detective #1- Nothing for me.

Detective #2- Thanks, I'm good, too.

Detective #1- So how are you holding up, Mrs. Stevenson?

Carlotta- I am hanging in there.

Detective #1- Our condolences to you and your family. Michael was a great person.

Carlotta- Thank you. You knew my husband?

Detective- We go way back, your husband saved my life. Plus he had done so much for the community.

Carlotta- That is good to know.

Detective #2- How did you meet Michael?

Carlotta- (smiles as she remembers) I first met in him in Law school thirty years ago. He was married at the time and I was engaged. After graduate school, we lost contact. Then when I moved to California, our paths crossed again.

Detective #1- So what happened when you met up with him?

Carlotta- He told me that he was recently divorced and had retired from practicing law. We just talked; we were old friends catching up.

Detective #2- How did it go from friendship to marriage?

Carlotta- It just happened, neither one of us were thinking of marriage. He had recently gotten out of a bitter divorce and I was there for him as a friend, years later he asked me to be his wife.

Detective #2- How do you know it was a bitter divorce?

Carlotta- That is what he told me.

Detective #1- Who do you think killed him?

Carlotta- (begins to cry) I don't know, I do not know who would want to do such a terrible thing.

Detective #1- Sorry ma'am we did not mean to upset you.

Detective #1- Did he have any enemies you knew of? Anyone hated him?

Carlotta- Not that I am aware of.

Detective #2- Okay thank you for your time. That is all the questions we have.

Detective #1- Have a good evening.

Carlotta- You both do the same.

The Detectives walk back to their car.

Detective #1- What did you think of her?

Detective #2- She seemed genuine.

Scene 23

There is a trial going on.

The state of California vs. Kim Stevenson. Kim is being tried for the murder of her ex husband. Everyone thinks Kim killed her husband. They had a bitter divorce and she threatened him on numerous occasions. Kim has maintained her innocence. Brandon is a junior in college. Sasha is a high school senior. Brandon visits when he can, he has been at his mother's side during the trial. Kim's parents Teddy and Stephanie have been at her side too, supporting her; two of her brothers are there as well, Kevin and Anthony. Her best friends Karen, Monisha and Sharon are all there in court as well to support Kim.

There are hundreds and hundreds of camera crews outside the courthouse, it's mayhem. Inside, the courthouse is packed to capacity, there is a lot of talking in the courtroom. Judge Tom Williams is residing.

Judge Williams- (Hits his gavel) Order! Order in the court please. I am going to tell you all once the rules of my courtroom. Please pay attention because if you fail to obey the rules you will be escorted out. There will be no yelling, shouting or screaming out in the courtroom. When the defense and presecutors call their witnesses, you are not to make any loud smart comments. Please just be professional. The State of California vs. Kim Stevenson. I am ready for opening statements. I will hear from the prosecutor first.

> The prosecutor is a black female, her name is Kelly Morris.

Prosecutor- Judge Williams and members of the court, we are here today because the life of a respected, popular and well love retired lawyer was murdered in a senseless, calculating and ruthless way. He was murdered on his wedding day.

Carlotta- (screams out loud) Oh God!

Judge Williams- Mrs. Stevenson are you okay? Do we need to take a break?

Carlotta- No, your Honor, I'm sorry please proceed.

Judge Williams- Please continue.

Prosecutor- Michael was gunned down by his ex-wife (she points to Kim) who hated the fact that he divorced her. Moreover, Kim Stevenson hated the fact that he was remarrying. When Michael Stevenson told his wife he wanted a divorce, she accused him of having an affair and she felt that was the reason he was leaving. Kim threatened her husband not once, or twice she threatened him on numerous occasions. Records will show that Ms. Stevenson hired a private investigator to follow her husband's every move not for a few months, but for four long years. She never found anything on him; he was not with another woman. But Kim Stevenson was not satisfied and she vowed to make his life a living hell, and a living hell is what she made it. Mr. Stevenson was going through was a middle-age crisis. He was deeply depressed and troubled; he was confused and if his wife had only supported him, he would have come back to her. But instead, she made his life a living hell. He was getting counseling for his issues and his psychiatrist is here today to speak on his behalf. We have all been there, we have all been a little depressed at times, and asking ourselves the question is this all life has to offer. Well that is what was happening to Michael. Kim threatened to keep the kids away from him, and you know why? Kim knew how much he loved those kids, and she knew it would kill him. She wanted to do just that. Michael told her that she could have everything. He told her he would continue to pay for everything; he did not want a messy divorce. Michael apologized to Kim saying he was sorry and never meant to hurt her. The man was having a nervous breakdown but did she did not care. Kim only cared about herself; she is cold, selfish and ruthless. Kim made the divorce messy, she tried to kill him on numerous occasions and the tapes will show that Kim stabbed him on more than one occasion. The day her divorce was final, Kim rushed to Michael and began yelling, screaming and punching him and had to be restrained by the guards. She was yelling I am going to kill you! You are a dead man Michael! Michael did not press charges because he still loved his wife. Kim finally succeeded in killing Michael. Kim was the one who pulled the trigger. I will tell you how and why as the case unfolds. Kim broke all of the rules. Michael won joint custody of the kids but he rarely ever saw the kids. Kim and her parents made sure of that. The bitter divorce and the fact that he could not see his kids sent Michael into a more depressed state. Michael was crushed and went into seclusion, he never stopped going to counseling, and he wanted to die. He loved his family, and despite the fact that he wanted a divorce he loved Kim and the kids. Then he finally ran into a good friend with whom he went to school and she helped him get himself together. They were friends in college and rekindled that friendship. The friendship grew into love and he wanted to marry this woman because he found love again. Michael found someone he could trust and love, someone he could enjoy life with, but he never got a chance to make her his wife because he was murdered during his wedding ceremony.

Carlotta- (Cries out loud again as she holds her baby) Oh God! Oh God! Ooooh. OOoh. (she is sobbing)

> Carlotta's sister grabs the baby and consoles her. Tears are running down Stephanie's face, Teddy consoles her.

Prosecutor- (The prosecutor continues talking, she walks closer towards the jurors and family members and says) Michael was shot twice. Kim aimed directly at his heart. The bullets pierced his heart and there was no way he was going to survive. It was a cold, calculated murder. Kim meant to kill him; leaving him to die in the church in the arms of his soon to be wife. How heartless? How sick? How senseless and horrific? Many would probably ask how? Well I will tell you how, she was a woman scorned. Kim believed that until death do us part, if I can't have you, no one else will. She told Michael that on many occasions. She had a good man and she did not know how to take care of him when he needed her the most. So maybe he said the wrong things, maybe he should not have said he wanted a divorce, maybe he should have chosen better words; maybe he should have said he needed some time to himself, because truly that is all he needed. Michael was depressed and confused and said he wanted a divorce. He made it very clear that there was no other woman. Michael told Kim that it was not about her, he was the one with the problem. Kim was not interested in hearing that. Kim told everyone who would listen that her husband left her for another woman, and she was the poor wife being the victim, when in fact he was the victim. Remember that Kim hired a private detective to have him followed for four years, and there was no other woman. He was living in a hotel going back and forth to counseling. Kim Stevenson is an evil, selfish, and scorned woman; don't let her appearance today looking and acting like the victim, fool you. Kim murdered her husband and now his kids, Brandon, Sasha and Michael Jr. are fatherless because of her act. Take a good look at her, think about how he died and think about his widow. Think about the kids. Think about Michael's parents and his sisters. Thank you for your time. (The prosecutor takes her seat)

Judge Williams- Defense attorney, your opening statements please.

Jack Stoker Defense Attorney- Good morning Judge Williams, jurors, family and friends. This is truly a tragedy and no one is disputing that, however what I am disputing is Kim Stevenson did not murder her husband. The real killer is still out there. Yes she is an easy suspect because she was married to him and then he left her for whatever the reason. Of course she was hurt and angry, wouldn't you be if your marriage of 18 years came down to your husband saying I want a divorce? Then he does not give you a reason; he just says he wants out. (Defense Attorney Stoker walks closer to the jurors) Put yourself in Kim's shoes, how would you have reacted? Be very honest with yourselves. We all know most times when a man asks for a divorce there is another woman in the picture. Let's not pretend that is usually not the case. Kim did ask Michael why he was leaving her. Michael gave her no specific reasons other than he was going through something and he wanted out. Kim needed to know exactly why. Instead he said he just wants out, he does not know why he just wants out. I don't know about you, but if my wife came home and told me suddenly that she wanted a divorce, with no explanations other than I want out, I am going through something. I would be livid. I would lose my mind. It was a loving marriage; they were together a total of twenty two years including their dating years, two beautiful kids, and the quintessential marriage that everyone wanted. They communicated well, they travelled together, they did almost everything together, and they were a true family. Yeah think to yourselves, how you would have reacted. Let me tell you how Kim reacted. How she felt. Kim was deeply hurt, she was angry as expected, she could not believe what she was hearing, she felt betrayed, cheated and yes, she believed it was another woman. How could she help him when his response was I just want out of this marriage? What is a wife to do? Let me tell you all what led Kim into a deep depression. Kim's doctor is here, her kids are here and they will tell you how close to death Kim came. Kim was literally suffering and dying of a broken heart. Now I know that sounds like a cliché to most of you, but I am telling you, Kim Stevenson loved her husband more than life itself, she would have given her life for him. So when he told her he wanted out with no other explanations she got depressed. Each time she thought of him not being there with her, her heart literally hurt, let me repeat, her heart literally hurt. She loved him and if he had asked her for help she would have helped. So before you go judging Kim, put yourself in her position and be honest with yourself and see how you would have reacted. Kim Stevenson did not kill her ex-husband. She is being accused of an unspeakable crime that she did not commit, and I am here to prove that on the day Mr. Stevenson was killed, Kim was home with her kids. She cannot be in two places at one time. You will see phone records of conversation Kim was having with her mother during the time her ex-husband was shot. The real killer is out there and I will prove that you are trying the wrong person today. Thanks for your time.

Judge Williams- (looks to the Prosecutor) Please call your first witness.

Prosecutor- I call Paula Medley to the stand.

Paula goes to the stand.

Prosecutor- Please have a seat. Tell us how you know the defendant and her husband.

Paula- I am her neighbor, I have been her neighbor since they moved in twenty years ago and I spy on them every now and then.

Prosecutor- Were you two close?

Paula- Hell, no.

Prosecutor- Why do you say it like that Mrs. Medley?

Paula- Call me Paula or Ms. Medley I am divorced now.

Prosecutor- Sorry to hear that; please answer the question Ms. Medley.

Paula- No, we were not friends. Kim thought she was too good for people; she was very snobbish. She ignored me so I ignored her too.

Prosecutor- So you were never invited over for cookouts, parties any of that?

Paula- No. Even if I was, I would not have gone, she is too snobbish.

Prosecutor- Have you ever heard fights or any guns shots at the Stevenson house?

Paula- Yes, I have heard a gun go off one time and that was it.

Defense Attorney Stoker- Objection, these questions are unnecessary.

Judge- Sustained. Jurors, please disregard the last question from the prosecution. Continue

Prosecutor- Thanks. No further questions.

Judge Williams- (turns to defense attorney) Do you have any questions for this witness?

Defense Attorney Stoker- Yes.   Ms. Medley you testified earlier that you spy on the Stevensons all the time, and you know their every move, is that correct?

Paula- Yes, that is correct. I see when they are going out and when they are coming in.

Defense Attorney Stoker- So on May 12, did you see Ms. Stevenson leave her house?

Paula - She never left her house that day.

Defense Attorney Stoker- And how do you know that?

Paula- Because I was sitting outside when the pizza guy came to the door and I saw Kim. She never left the house.

Defense Attorney Stoker- Thank you, no further questions.

Judge Williams- You may step down. (he looks at to the prosecutor and says) Please call your next witness.

Prosecutor calls Brandon to the stand.

Prosecutor- Brandon how are you doing?

Brandon- Fine.

Prosecutor- Describe the marriage of your parents to us.

Brandon- My parents had a good marriage, we went on many family vacations. Both my parents were loving and great parents.

Prosecutor- How did you feel when your parents divorced?

Brandon- I was devastated. I could not understand why. I was deeply hurt.

Prosecutor- Did you ever hear your parents fight?

Brandon- Yes.

Prosecutor- Have you ever heard your mom threaten to kill your dad?

Defense Stoker- Objection your honor this is hear say.

Judge Williams- Overruled. Please answer the question Brandon.

Brandon- Yes.

Prosecutor- Thanks no further questions?

Judge Williams- (looks over at Defense Attorney Stoker and asks) Do you have any questions for the witness?

Defense Attorney Stoker- Yes. How are you doing Brandon?

Brandon- Good.

Defense Attorney Stoker- Who was home when the pizza arrived?

Brandon- My mom, my sister and me.

Defense Attorney Stoker- How many times have you heard your mom threaten to kill your dad?

Brandon- Only once and that is because she was drinking and they were having an argument.

Defense Attorney Stoker- Thanks Brandon. No further questions.

Judge Williams- You may go back to your seat. Please call your next witness.

Defense Attorney Stoker- I call Dr. Jenkins to the stand.

Dr. Jenkins walks to the stand.

Defense Attorney Stoker- What was your relationship with Mr. Stevenson?

Dr. Jenkins- He was my patient.

Defense Attorney Stoker- What was he your patient for?

Dr. Jenkins- Mr. Stevenson was having a nervous breakdown; he was also suffering from depression while going through a middle-age crisis.

Defense Attorney- Mr. Stoker, describe to everyone how that can affect a person?

Dr. Jenkins- He felt trapped. He felt that everyone needed him and he did not have time for himself. He felt he was a failure to his family, because sometimes his cases took him away from family dinners, he felt guilty when he won cases and when the other family lost, he felt their pain. Michael felt he had no time for himself and he felt the weight of the world coming down on him. He felt pain and guilt because he had a twin brother who was incarcerated for double homicide, Michael refused to be his lawyer and his little brother was sentenced to life, he committed suicide two days later. Michael never forgave himself for that. Michael was fighting those demons. Some of his family members hated him. They felt he was living the "rich life", while his siblings were living mediocre. I think Michael just needed some time alone that's all.

Defense Attorney Stoker - Do you have the video of Michael during his sessions?

Prosecutor- Objection, Your Honor that is not necessary.

Defense Attorney Stoker - Its absolutely necessary, this way you can see Michael tell the doctor in his own words, that way no one can say it's hear say.

Judge Williams- Objection overruled go ahead doctor Jenkins, let us see the video.

Dr. Jenkins plays one of the videos, this is the first session when Michael is talking about his problems.

Dr. Jenkins- How are you doing today Michael?

Michael- Not so good.

Dr. Jenkins- Tell me about it.

Michael- I told my wife I wanted a divorce and of course she went ballistic.

Dr. Jenkins- What do you mean?

Michael- She said I could never leave her. She thought I was leaving her for another woman.

Dr. Jenkins- Are you?

Michael- No, I would never do that.

Dr. Jenkins- Did you explain to your wife the reason you wanted to leave?

Michael- I tried but she did not believe me. I guess I don't blame her. I just said I want out. I did not give her a reason. I did not know what to say really. I needed to be alone.

Dr. Jenkins- Why didn't you say that?

Michael- Because I am not sure how much time alone I really needed. It could have been a week a month or even longer.

Dr. Jenkins- Tell me about your job.

Michael- Well I am a prosecutor and I deal with very high level cases. Corruption, murder, and spies you name it.

Dr. Jenkins- Do you have a lot of enemies?

Michael- (smiles) I have more enemies than I have friends. I have a dangerous job.

Dr. Jenkins- Why do you think some people hate you?

Michael- I would not say they hate me per se, however they hate my profession. I've never lost a case. I've put away many high ranking folks so I am hated for that.

Dr. Jenkins- Are you concerned for your life?

Michael- All the time, but that is the profession that I have chosen so I take my chances. I do have body guards for protection.

Defense Attorney Stoker- Okay we are going to stop the video. Okay you have heard Michael say in his own words that he has enemies due to his profession. Anyone could have killed Michael. I have no further questions for this witness.

> Dr. Jenkins leaves the stand.

Judge Williams- Please call your next witness.

Defense Stoker- I call Kim Stevenson to the stand.

> Kim walks to the stand, she seems a bit weak, and she is wearing a white pants suit with a green blouse inside. She gets to the witness stand.

Defense Attorney Stoker- How are you doing today Ms. Stevenson?

Kim- I am hanging in there, thanks for asking. Please call me Kim.

Defense Attorney Stoker- Let us just get this out of the bag right now, did you kill your husband?

Kim- (crying) No I did not.

Defense Attorney Stoker- Do you know who might have?

Kim- No.

Defense Attorney Stoker- Have you ever made threats to your husband?

Kim- Yes, in anger but I did not mean it.

Defense Attorney Stoker- Tell us about your marriage, how long were you all married and how did you meet?

Kim- (smiles as she reminisces) I met Michael at college during freshman orientation, he was a sophomore and I was a freshman. He was a football player. He came up to me and introduced himself. We talked for awhile and then exchanged numbers. We dated for two years and then got married; we had been together ever since.

Attorney Stoker- During your twenty something years together, have you all ever separated, went to counseling or had any problems in the marriage?

Kim- Never. Actually my friends would always say how envious they were of us. We were committed to each other and our kids. It was a great marriage.

Defense Attorney Stoker- That is why it was hard for you to comprehend when Michael said he wanted a divorce, correct?

Kim- Correct, I immediately thought it was another woman, because we were happy throughout our marriage and I could not understand why.

Defense Attorney Stoker- Kim on the day of your husband's murder please tell the jurors where you were.

Kim- (crying) I was at home with my kids, fixing a snack while they ordered pizza.

Defense Attorney Stoker- So let's see, according to the records Michael was killed around 2:00 pm that afternoon. When did your kids order the pizza?

Kim- They ordered the pizza at around 12:30 pm.

Defense Attorney Stoker- I have a receipt from Pizza Hut that the pizza was ordered at 12:30 pm. The delivery boy is here, he will testify if need be.

Judge Williams- I don't think that will be necessary.

Defense Attorney Stoker- Michael was shot at 2:00 pm; the pizza came at 1:30 pm. Kim could not have killed Michael in a 30 minute time frame. It's impossible. The wedding location was an hour and a half away from her house. Even if she drove at 70 mph it would not have been enough time. So there is the proof, Kim did not kill her husband, she did not have enough time to do that and get back home. She was at home with her kids. The cops searched the house; there was no murder weapon found, no blood. The prosecutor's case does not make sense. I have no further questions.

Judge Williams- Prosecutor do you have any other questions?

Prosecutor- Of course (she approaches the stand) Hello Ms. Stevenson, how are you doing today?

Kim- Fine thanks.

Prosecutor- When your husband came home that night and told you he wanted a divorce what did you do?

Kim- I was shocked and angry.

Prosecutor- Understood, but what did you do?

Kim- I yelled at him. I wanted to know why.

Prosecutor- What else did you do?

Kim- That was it.

Prosecutor- Ms. Stevenson, remember that you took an oath, what else did you do?

> Kim pauses, she looks at her attorney, her mother, her kids, Brandon and Sasha, and Michael's new wife Carlotta.

Kim- We argued.

Prosecutor- I got that part, but what happened while you were arguing?

Kim- (softly whispers) I grabbed a knife.

Prosecutor- I'm sorry I could not hear you, please speak up.

Kim- I grabbed a knife out of the drawer.

Prosecutor- So you grabbed a knife. Why? What were your intentions?

Kim- I said I was angry.

Defense Stoker- Objection, the prosecution is badgering the witness.

Judge Williams- Sustained, please continue.

Prosecutor- What were you trying to do with the knife?

> Kim begins to cry, the guard gives her a tissue.

Judge Williams- Ms. Stevenson, do you need a break?

Kim- No, I am fine.

Prosecutor- Please answer the question, what were your intentions when you grabbed the knife?

Kim- I wanted to scare him, I was angry and was drinking.

Prosecutor- You wanted to scare him, stab him or kill him? Which is it?

Defense Attorney Stoker- Objection Your Honor, she is badgering my witness.

Prosecutor- I am just trying to get clarity on what Kim's intentions were.

Judge Williams- Objection overruled continue.

Prosecutor- What were your intentions Ms. Stevenson?

Kim- I was angry and not thinking. I wanted to kill him, but I was not going to.

> The jurors gasp with a sound of ooh's and aah's,
> they are talking amongst themselves.

Judge Williams- (hits his gavel) Quiet in the court please.

Prosecutor- No further questions.

Judge Williams- Ms. Stevenson, you make take your seat. (looks at Defense Attorney Stoker and says) Please call your next witness.

Defense Attorney Stoker- Yes, I called Dr. Fenham to the stand, he is Kim's doctor.

> The doctor comes to the stand.

Defense Attorney Stoker- Please sit down Doctor. How are you today?

Dr. Fenham- Fine.

Defense Attorney Stoker- You are Kim's doctor and have been for twenty years, correct?

Dr. Fenham- That is correct. I helped her deliver those two wonderful kids. I knew the family pretty well. I was there for the kids' smallpocks and measles; you name it.

Defense Attorney Stoker- Describe Kim's mental and physical state prior to her divorce.

Dr. Fenham- She was extremely healthy. She got her physicals once a year. Kim ate healthy and was an avid runner. She was physically and mentally fine.

Defense Attorney Stoker- Was she on any medication?

Dr. Fenham- Never, however, after her husband asked her for a divorce she got depressed and had to be medicated.

Defense Attorney Stoker- Tell me about that?

Dr. Fenham- Kim took the news of divorce extremely hard. She stopped eating, and got extremely thin and weak. She went into shock. Her heart was literally broken; she had heart pains whenever she thought about the breakup, and she was deeply depressed. So I had to give her depression medication. Kim rarely took them because she is not used to taking medications. She became delirious.

Defense Attorney Stoker- What do you mean Doctor?

Dr. Fenham- Well she would hear things; she thought Michael was still living in the house. She would prepare his breakfast for him and then call out to him to come downstairs to eat the breakfast. She literally lost her mind. Kim passed out on many occasions and was deeply depressed. Her heart was truly broken. Her heart stopped at least on three occasions. She almost died.

Defense Attorney Stoker- How is she doing now Doctor?

Dr. Fenham- Well she has improved because she finally accepted the fact that Michael had moved on. Now I'm afraid that she is falling back into depression, because she has been accused of murder.

Defense Attorney Stoker- No further questions Your Honor.

Judge Williams- (looks at the prosecutor) Any questions?

Prosecutor- Yes of course. Dr. Fenham you said that Kim lost her mind there for a second, correct?

Dr. Fenham- Yes.

Prosecutor- So is it possible during that type of depression she could have killed her husband?

Defense Attorney Stoker- (jumps up) Objection Your Honor, this is crazy.

Judge Williams- Overruled. Please strike that question jurors.

Prosecutor- No further questions.

Judge Williams- (says to Defense Attorney Stoker) Do you have any other questions?

Defense Attorney Stoker- No Your Honor.

Judge Williams- Closing arguments please.

Prosecutor- This is an absolute tragedy and there are no winners here. Sasha, Brandon, and Michael, Jr. are without a father, thanks to Kim. This man was murdered, at his own wedding, in a church for crying out loud. It was a calculated murder; Kim knew he was getting married, and it hurt her that he was remarrying. So she killed him before the pastor could pronounce them man and wife. She was the only one with a motive. She had a lot at stake if he stayed single but even more if he died. Michael never changed his will after the divorce. However, he planned on doing so after he got married. Well Kim made sure of that by murdering him. Let me reiterate, if Michael died before he remarried she got everything. Kim murdered her husband in cold blood and I ask you find her guilty of murder on all counts. I recommend life in prison be given to her. Thank you.

Defense Attorney Stoker- Kim Stevenson did not kill her husband; you saw what time the pizza was delivered. The pizza delivery boy said he delivered the pizza to Ms. Stevenson. There is no way that Kim could have committed a murder in 30 minutes. The wedding location was 1 hour and a half away from her house. Yes Kim threatened to kill him on numerous occasions, but put yourself in her position, how would you feel? How would you react? This woman has lost her husband and has suffered tremendously; please do not take her away from her kids by locking her up for a murder she did not commit. The real killer is out there, it's not Kim Stevenson. Thank you.

Judge Williams- Thank you both. We will reconvene when a verdict is ready. This court is adjourned.

> Kim hugs her attorney and his assistant.

Kim- Thank you all so much for everything.

Defense Attorney Stoker- Go home and spend time with your kids and family. I do not want you to think about tomorrow okay. You are going to be fine. They are going to find you not guilty. I can feel it.

Kim- I will try, I wish I was as sure as you.

> They walk out of the courtroom, outside the courtroom Kim hugs Sasha and Brandon they walk out of the courthouse towards their car, it's a media frenzy, cameras, reporters, Kim's attorney is trying to get her through the crowd as reporters try to ask her questions.

Reporter #1- Ms. Stevenson did you kill your husband?

> Kim's attorney keeps pushing her through the crowd to get her to the limo.

Reporter #2- Do you know who did it?

Reporter #3- Do you think you will go to jail?

Reporter #4- Ms. Stevenson, Ms. Stevenson how did it go in there today?

Defense Attorney Stoker- Please no questions, please clear the way, Kim has nothing to say.

Reporter #4- (asks Prosecutor Morris) Mrs. Morris! Mrs. Morris! How did it go in there today?

Prosecutor- I have no comment; please get of my way, thank you.

> The cameras and reporters follow the prosecutor, Kim and her attorney to their cars, as the cars drive off, reporters are running behind the cars trying to take pictures and ask questions.
> Kim is dropped off in front of her house, there are already reporters waiting for her in front of the house.

Attorney Stoker- Okay I am going to walk you in, do not say anything to these reporters okay.

Kim- I want them gone.

Defense Stoker- If they are not on your property there is nothing you can do. So just walk in and say nothing.

Kim- Okay.

> Defense Stoker opens up the car door and ten reporters rush to him asking questions.

Defense Stoker- Please move away from the car, we have nothing to say.

> He holds Kim by the arm and walks her into her house, inside her family and friends are waiting for her.

Reporter #5- Ms Stevenson, did you kill your husband? How did it go in court today?

Defense Attorney Stoker- Please get off of her property. I will call the cops; my client has nothing to say.

> Kim walks into the house and her friends and family are cheering and clapping as she enters.

Teddy- You did great today, Honey.

Kim- Thanks Dad.

Kevin- We are all here for you. We have some food on the grill. There is chicken, turkey burgers, steak, macaroni and cheese, pasta ,etc. We are going to celebrate your victory.

Kim- Thanks everyone but the jurors are still deliberating and we haven't heard the verdict.

Sasha- We know Mom, but we are celebrating early.

Brandon- Let's all go out back and enjoy the food. You are going to be just fine.

> Everyone is in the backyard laughing, eating and having a good time. The phone rings. Teddy answers,

Teddy- Hello.

Defense Attorney Stoker- How are you Sir?

Teddy- I am good, what is going on?

Defense Attorney Stoker- Is Kim available?

Teddy- Yes but you can tell me.

Defense Attorney Stoker- The jurors have reached a verdict. So we have to be in court tomorrow. Tell Kim I will be there to pick her up at 8:30 am.

Teddy- Okay, thank you.

Stephanie- Who was it Teddy?

Teddy- The jurors have reached a verdict. We have to be in court tomorrow.

Kim- Oh my God! That was quick. What does that mean?

Teddy- Don't worry Honey, you are going to be okay.

Kim- Well it's 7 pm so we all need to get a good night's rest.

Karen- (walks over and hugs Kim) I will see you tomorrow.

Kim- (hugs her back) I love you. Thanks for your support, see you tomorrow.

Sharon- You know I love you Girl. I know you are innocent and you are going to be fine tomorrow. I am praying for you. See you tomorrow.

Kim- Love you Girl, thanks.

Monisha- I know you did not do it, I love you Girl. I will be there tomorrow.

Kim- Thanks Mo, love you too.

> Kim walks her friends to the door, she waves to them as they leave. She then goes into the back-yard and joins her family.

Teddy- Are you okay Honey?

Kim- Yes Dad.

Teddy- We are all going to stay over here tonight with you.

Kim- Thanks Dad. I appreciate that.

Stephanie- Okay let's clean up it's getting late and we all have an early day tomorrow.

> Everyone cleans up and then gather in the living room. Stephanie begins to cry.

Kim- Mom what is it?

Stephanie- I am happy to see my entire family together being supportive. This is what it's all about family. At the end of the day no matter what happens we are all a family.

Kevin- (gets up and hugs her) Oh Mom. You are the strength of this family. You are the glue that keeps us together.

Teddy- You are right Son. (Teddy walks over and hugs Kevin) I am so sorry for ever hurting you. You are my son and I love you.

Kevin- Thanks Dad. I needed to hear that.

Kim- Aaah that is so beautiful. You all are going to make me cry.

Stephanie- Me too.

Kim- Where are the kids?

Kevin- I think they went upstairs.

Stephanie- Okay we have a long day tomorrow. I think we should call it a night.

Kevin- I agree.

Kim- Good night everyone, see you all in the morning.

THE NEXT DAY JUDGMENT DAY

Kim is downstairs in the kitchen drinking some orange juice; Sasha comes in and gives her a hug.

Sasha- Good morning Mom how are you doing?

Kim- Nervous.

Sasha- Me too, I could not sleep last night.

Kim- Yes, me neither.

      Brandon comes into the kitchen.

Brandon- Hi Mom, how are you doing? Did you sleep well?

Kim- I got a little rest. What about you Son?

Brandon- I am hanging in there. I just want you to know that you are going to be okay today.

Kim- Thanks Son.

      Stephanie, Teddy, Kevin, Anthony walk into the kitchen.

Sasha- It's one big happy family.

Teddy- That is right, and that is how it will continue to be.

Kim- Anyone care for breakfast? There is fruit, French toast and pancakes.

Kevin- I will have some fruit.

Kim- What time is it?

Teddy- 8:20 am.

Kim- My attorney is going to pick me up in ten minutes. Gosh this is so nerve racking.

Teddy- It's going to be okay Sweetie.

> Kim's cells rings and she jumps at the sound of it.

Stephanie- You okay Dear?

Kim- Yes.

> Kim answers the phone,

Kim- Hello.

Defense Attorney Stoker- How are you doing this morning Kim?

Kim- Okay.

Defense Attorney Stoker- Great! I am outside, are you ready?

Kim- Yes, I will be right out.

Kim- My attorney is outside, are you all ready?

Teddy- We will follow behind the car.

Kim- Okay let's go.

Everyone walks outside, some neighbors are waving, some are giving thumbs up, and some are just staring.

Kim waves to them and so do the kids. They all get into the car and head to the courthouse. As they pull up to the courthouse about a thousand reporters, camera crews, and TV stations are waiting at the courthouse, it's all over the TV on every channel. As Kim's limo pulls up, the reporters flock to the car, Kim is scared. Her defense attorney calls the twenty police officers he hired to help escort them through the crowd to the courthouse.

Defense Attorney Stoker makes a call.

Cop #1- Hello Sir, are you ready for us?

Defense Attorney Stoker- Yes. It's mayhem out here. I want Kim and her family protected and escorted to and from the courthouse today.

Cop #1- We are on our way.

Two minutes later, twenty cops arrive telling the reporters and camera crews to back away from Kim's limo.

Police Officer Gary- Move away from the cars, if you do not move you will be arrested on the spot.

The crowd of reporters begins moving away from the car. Kim, her attorney and family are escorted into the courthouse by five cops. Kim and her attorney enters the courthouse, the guards and the prosecutor are already there. The courthouse is packed.

Kim- I am so nervous.

Defense Attorney Stoker- Relax Kim, it's going to be okay.

Judge Williams- (enters the courtroom) Good morning everyone. This court is now in session. Let me repeat the rules, because I do not want to have to put a beat down on anyone. I will ask the jurors for their verdict. One of the jurors will read the verdict and we will proceed accordingly. Regardless of the outcome, any looting, fighting, riots, cursing, or acting out other than in a professional manner, will cause you to be arrested, no questions asked. I will not stand for any craziness in my courtroom. (he then ask the jurors) Have you reached a verdict?

Juror #1- Yes Your Honor we have.

Judge Williams- Please read the verdict.

Juror #1- We the jury find the defendant Kim Allison Stevenson not guilty of first degree murder of her husband. Aggravated assault. Not guilty.

> Kim's friends and family are cheering and clapping.

Kim- (puts her hands in the air and says) Thank You God, she immediately hugs her attorney.

Defense Attorney Stoker- I am so happy for you.

Prosecutor- (is angry) She folds her briefcase and walks over to Michael's family and says) I am so sorry.

> Kim's entire family screams out loud saying yeah, they are hugging each other, crying as they hug each other.

Judge Williams- (hits his gavel) Order! Order in the courtroom! The jurors have made their decision. Ms. Stevenson you are cleared of all charges, this court is adjourned.

Kim- (hugs her attorney again) Thank you! Thank you so much.

Defense Attorney Stoker- Don't mention it, just go and enjoy your life.

> The cops surround Kim and her family. They are escorted out of the courtroom. As they exit the courthouse reporters begin to ask questions.

Reporter #5- (talking to Kim) Ms. Stevenson how do you feel?

Kim- I feel great.

Reporter #6- Who do you think did it?

Kim- I do not know.

Reporter #7- (talking to Attorney Stoker) What did you think sealed your case?

Attorney Stoker- We proved that Kim was at home during the time of the murder.

Reporter #6- Who do you think killed Michael?

Attorney Stoker- I have no idea.

Reporter #8- So what happens now?

Attorney Stoker- I go home to my family.

Reporter #9- (asking the prosecutor) What are your comments regarding the verdict?

Prosecutor- I have no comment.

Reporter #10- Do you think Kim got way with murder?

Prosecutor- Yes.

NEXT MORNING

Two students are sitting in a diner reading the newspaper.

Guy #1- (says to the other) Did you see the verdict on the Stevenson case?

Guy #2- Yeah Man I see, that is wild. He actually got away with it.

Guy#1- Yes he did.

Guy #2- I knew he would.

The screen shows Brandon the next day walking on the campus of his college, going to class.

The End

www.ingramcontent.com/pod-product-compliance
Lightning Source LLC
Chambersburg PA
CBHW030924120626
46554CB00001B/268